RAGGEDY ANN
STORIES

Written & Illustrated by
JOHNNY GRUELLE

LITTLE SIMON
New York   London   Toronto   Sydney

LITTLE SIMON

An imprint of Simon & Schuster Children's Publishing Division

1230 Avenue of the Americas, New York, New York 10020

Afterword copyright © 1993 by Kim Gruelle

LITTLE SIMON is a registered trademark of Simon & Schuster, Inc., and associated colophon is a trademark of Simon & Schuster, Inc.

Manufactured in the United States of America

First Little Simon edition, 2005

10 9 8 7 6 5 4 3 2 1

ISBN 1-4169-0982-6

Raggedy Ann Stories and *Raggedy Andy Stories* were previously published individually by Simon & Schuster Books for Young Readers and were previously catalogued individually by the Library of Congress.

PREFACE AND DEDICATION

AS I write this, I have before me on my desk, propped up against the telephone, an old rag doll. Dear old Raggedy Ann!

The same Raggedy Ann with which my mother played when a child.

There she sits, a trifle loppy and loose-jointed, looking me squarely in the face in a straightforward, honest manner, a twinkle where her shoe-button eyes reflect the electric light.

Evidently Raggedy has been to a "tea party" today, for her face is covered with chocolate.

She smiles happily and continuously.

True, she has been nibbled by mice, who have made nests out of the soft cotton with which she has been stuffed, but Raggedy smiled just as broadly when the mice nibbled at her, for her smile is painted on.

What adventures you must have had, Raggedy!

What joy and happiness you have brought into this world!

And no matter what treatment you have received, how patient you have been!

What lessons of kindness and fortitude you might teach could you but talk; you with your wisdom of fifty-nine years. No wonder Rag Dolls are the best beloved! You are so kindly, so patient, so lovable.

The more you become torn, tattered and loose-jointed, Rag Dolls, the more you are loved by children.

Who knows but that Fairyland is filled with old, lovable Rag Dolls—soft, loppy Rag Dolls who ride through all the wonders of Fairyland in the crook of dimpled arms, snuggling close to childish breasts within which beat hearts filled with eternal sunshine.

So, to the millions of children and grown-ups who have loved a Rag Doll, I dedicate these stories of Raggedy Ann.

JOHNNY GRUELLE.

INTRODUCTION

Marcella liked to play up in the attic at Grandma's quaint old house, 'way out in the country, for there were so many old forgotten things to find up there.

One day when Marcella was up in the attic and had played with the old spinning wheel until she had grown tired of it, she curled up on an old horse-hair sofa to rest.

"I wonder what is in that barrel, 'way back in the corner?" she thought, as she jumped from the sofa and climbed over two dusty trunks to the barrel standing back under the eaves.

It was quite dark back there, so when Marcella had pulled a large bundle of things from the barrel she took them over to the dormer window where she could see better. There was a funny little bonnet with long white ribbons. Marcella put it on.

In an old leather bag she found a number of tin-types of queer looking men and women in old-fashioned clothes. And there was one picture of a very pretty little girl with long curls tied tightly back from her forehead and wearing a long dress and queer pantaloons which reached to her shoe-tops. And then out of the heap she pulled an old rag doll with only one shoe-button eye and a painted nose and a smiling mouth. Her dress was of soft material, blue with pretty little flowers and dots all over it.

Forgetting everything else in the happiness of her find, Marcella caught up the rag doll and ran downstairs to show it to Grandma.

"Well! Well! Where did you find it?" Grandma cried. "It's old Raggedy Ann!" she went on as she hugged the doll to her breast. "I had forgotten her. She has been in the attic for fifty years, I guess! Well! Well! Dear old Raggedy Ann! I will sew another button on her right away!" and Grandma went to the machine drawer and got her needle and thread.

Marcella watched the sewing while Grandma told how she had played with Raggedy Ann when she was a little girl.

"Now!" Grandma laughed, "Raggedy Ann, you have two fine shoe-button eyes and with them you can see the changes that have taken place in the world while you have been shut up so long in the attic! For, Raggedy Ann, you have a new playmate and mistress now, and I hope you both will have as much happiness together as you and I used to have!"

Then Grandma gave Raggedy Ann to Marcella, saying very seriously, "Marcella, let me introduce my very dear friend, Raggedy Ann. Raggedy, this is my grand-daughter, Marcella!" And Grandma gave the doll a twitch with her fingers in such a way that the rag doll nodded her head to Marcella.

"Oh, Grandma! Thank you ever and ever so much!" Marcella cried as she gave Grandma a hug and kiss. "Raggedy Ann and I will have just loads of fun."

And this is how Raggedy Ann joined the doll family at Marcella's house, where she began the adventures of Raggedy Ann, told in the following stories.

RAGGEDY ANN LEARNS A LESSON

One day the dolls were left all to themselves.

Their little mistress had placed them all around the room and told them to be nice children while she was away.

And there they sat and never even so much as wiggled a finger, until their mistress had left the room.

Then the soldier dolly turned his head and solemnly winked at Raggedy Ann.

And when the front gate clicked and the dollies knew they were alone in the house, they all scrambled to their feet.

"Now let's have a good time!" cried the tin soldier. "Let's all go in search of something to eat!"

"Yes! Let's all go in search of something to eat!" cried all the other dollies.

"When Mistress had me out playing with her this morning," said Raggedy Ann, "she carried me by a door near the back of the house and I smelled something which smelled as if it would taste delicious!"

"Then you lead the way, Raggedy Ann!" cried the French dolly.

"I think it would be a good plan to elect Raggedy Ann as our leader on this expedition!" said the Indian doll.

At this all the other dolls clapped their hands together and shouted, "Hurrah! Raggedy Ann will be our leader."

So Raggedy Ann, very proud indeed to have the confidence and love of all the other dollies, said that she would be very glad to be their leader.

"Follow me!" she cried as her wobbly legs carried her across the floor at a lively pace.

The other dollies followed, racing about the house until they came to the pantry door. "This is the place!" cried Raggedy Ann, and sure enough, all the dollies smelled something which they knew must be very good to eat.

But none of the dollies was tall enough to open the door and, although they pushed and pulled with all their might, the door remained tightly closed.

The dollies were talking and pulling and pushing and every once in a while one would fall over and the others would step on her in their efforts to open the door. Finally Raggedy Ann drew away from the others and sat down on the floor.

When the other dollies discovered Raggedy Ann sitting there, running her rag hands through her yarn hair, they knew she was thinking.

"Sh! Sh!" they said to each other and quietly went over near Raggedy Ann and sat down in front of her.

"There must be a way to get inside," said Raggedy Ann.

"Raggedy says there must be a way to get inside!" cried all the dolls.

"I can't seem to think clearly to-day," said Raggedy Ann. "It feels as if my head were ripped."

At this the French doll ran to Raggedy Ann and took off her bonnet. "Yes, there is a rip in your head, Raggedy!" she said and pulled a pin from her skirt and pinned up Raggedy's head. "It's not a very neat job, for I got some puckers in it!" she said.

"Oh that is ever so much better!" cried Raggedy Ann. "Now I can think quite clearly."

"Now Raggedy can think quite clearly!" cried all the dolls.

"My thoughts must have leaked out the rip before!" said Raggedy Ann.

JOHNNY GRUELLE

"They must have leaked out before, dear Raggedy!" cried all the other dolls.

"Now that I can think so clearly," said Raggedy Ann, "I think the door must be locked and to get in we must unlock it!"

"That will be easy!" said the Dutch doll who says "Mamma" when he is tipped backward and forward, "For we will have the brave tin soldier shoot the key out of the lock!"

"I can easily do that!" cried the tin soldier, as he raised his gun.

"Oh, Raggedy Ann!" cried the French dolly. "Please do not let him shoot!"

"No!" said Raggedy Ann. "We must think of a quieter way!"

After thinking quite hard for a moment, Raggedy Ann jumped up and said: "I have it!" And she caught up the Jumping Jack and held him up to the door; then Jack slid up his stick and unlocked the door.

Then the dollies all pushed and the door swung open.

My! Such a scramble! The dolls piled over one another in their desire to be the first at the goodies.

They swarmed upon the pantry shelves and in their eagerness spilled a pitcher of cream which ran all over the French dolly's dress.

The Indian doll found some corn bread and dipping it in the molasses he sat down for a good feast.

A jar of raspberry jam was overturned and the dollies ate of this until their faces were all purple.

The tin soldier fell from the shelf three times and bent one of his tin legs, but he scrambled right back up again.

Never had the dolls had so much fun and excitement, and they had all eaten their fill when they heard the click of the front gate.

They did not take time to climb from the shelves, but all rolled or jumped off to the floor and scrambled back to their

room as fast as they could run, leaving a trail of bread crumbs and jam along the way.

Just as their mistress came into the room the dolls dropped in whatever positions they happened to be in.

"This is funny!" cried Mistress. "They were all left sitting in their places around the room! I wonder if Fido has been shaking them up!" Then she saw Raggedy Ann's face and picked her up. "Why Raggedy Ann, you are all sticky! I do believe you are covered with jam!" and Mistress tasted Raggedy Ann's hand. "Yes! It's JAM! Shame on you, Raggedy Ann! You've been in the pantry and all the others, too!" and with this the dolls' mistress dropped Raggedy Ann on the floor and left the room.

When she came back she had on an apron and her sleeves were rolled up.

She picked up all the sticky dolls and putting them in a basket she carried them out under the apple tree in the garden.

There she had placed her little tub and wringer and she took the dolls one at a time, and scrubbed them with a scrubbing brush and soused them up and down and this way and that in the soap suds until they were clean.

Then she hung them all out on the clothes-line in the sunshine to dry.

There the dolls hung all day, swinging and twisting about as the breeze swayed the clothes-line.

"I do believe she scrubbed my face so hard she wore off my smile!" said Raggedy Ann, after an hour of silence.

JOHNNY GRUELLE

"No, it is still there!" said the tin solder, as the wind twisted him around so he could see Raggedy. "But I do believe my arms will never work without squeaking, they feel so rusted," he added.

Just then the wind twisted the little Dutch doll and loosened his clothes-pin, so that he fell to the grass below with a sawdusty bump and as he rolled over he said, "Mamma!" in a squeaky voice.

Late in the afternoon the back door opened and the little mistress came out with a table and chairs. After setting the table she took all the dolls from the line and placed them about the table.

They had lemonade with grape jelly in it, which made it a beautiful lavender color, and little "Baby-teeny-weeny-cookies" with powdered sugar on them.

After this lovely dinner, the dollies were taken in the house, where they had their hair brushed and nice clean nighties put on.

Then they were placed in their beds and Mistress kissed each one good night and tiptoed from the room.

All the dolls lay as still as mice for a few minutes, then Raggedy Ann raised up on her cotton-stuffed elbows and said: "I have been thinking!"

"Sh!" said all the other dollies, "Raggedy has been thinking!"

"Yes," said Raggedy Ann, "I have been thinking; our mistress gave us the nice dinner out under the trees to teach us a lesson. She wished us to know that we could have had all the goodies we wished, whenever we wished, if we had behaved ourselves. And our lesson was that we must never take without asking what we could always have for the asking! So let us all remember and try never again to do anything which might cause those who love us any unhappiness!"

"Let us all remember," chimed all the other dollies.

And Raggedy Ann, with a merry twinkle in her shoe-button eyes, lay back in her little bed, her cotton head filled with thoughts of love and happiness.

RAGGEDY ANN AND THE WASHING

"Why, Dinah! How could you!"

Mamma looked out of the window and saw Marcella run up to Dinah and take something out of her hand and then put her head in her arm and commence crying.

"What is the trouble, Dear?" Mamma asked, as she came out the door and knelt beside the little figure shaking with sobs.

Marcella held out Raggedy Ann. But such a comical looking Raggedy Ann!

Mamma had to smile in spite of her sympathy, for Raggedy Ann looked ridiculous!

Dinah's big eyes rolled out in a troubled manner, for Marcella had snatched Raggedy Ann from Dinah's hand as she cried, "Why, Dinah! How could you?"

Dinah could not quite understand and, as she dearly loved Marcella, she was troubled.

Raggedy Ann was not in the least downhearted and while she felt she must look very funny she continued to smile, but with a more expansive smile than ever before.

Raggedy Ann knew just how it all happened and her remaining shoe-button eye twinkled.

She remembered that morning when Marcella came to the

nursery to take the nighties from the dolls and dress them she had been cross.

Raggedy Ann thought at the time "Perhaps she had climbed out of bed backwards!" For Marcella complained to each doll as she dressed them.

And when it came Raggedy's time to be dressed, Marcella was very cross for she had scratched her finger on a pin when dressing the French doll.

So, when Marcella heard the little girl next door calling to her, she ran out of the nursery and gave Raggedy Ann a toss from her as she ran.

Now it happened Raggedy lit in the clothes hamper and there she lay all doubled up in a knot.

A few minutes afterwards Dinah came through the hall with an armful of clothes and piled them in the hamper on top of Raggedy Ann.

Then Dinah carried the hamper out in back of the house where she did the washing.

Dinah dumped all the clothes into the boiler and poured water on them.

The boiler was then placed upon the stove.

When the water began to get warm, Raggedy Ann wiggled around and climbed up amongst the clothes to the top of the boiler to peek out. There was too much steam and she could see nothing. For that matter, Dinah could not see Raggedy Ann, either, on account of the steam.

So Dinah, using an old broom handle, stirred the clothes in the boiler and the clothes and Raggedy Ann were stirred and whirled around until all were thoroughly boiled.

When Dinah took the clothes a piece at a time from the boiler and scrubbed them, she finally came upon Raggedy Ann.

Now Dinah did not know but that Marcella had placed Raggedy in the clothes hamper to be washed, so she soaped Raggedy well and scrubbed her up and down over the rough wash-board.

Two buttons from the back of Raggedy's dress came off

and one of Raggedy Ann's shoe-button eyes was loosened as Dinah gave her face a final scrub.

Then Dinah put Raggedy Ann's feet in the wringer and turned the crank. It was hard work getting Raggedy through the wringer, but Dinah was very strong. And of course it happened! Raggedy Ann came through as flat as a pancake.

It was just then, that Marcella returned and saw Raggedy.

"Why, Dinah! How could you!" Marcella had sobbed as she snatched the flattened Raggedy Ann from the bewildered Dinah's hand.

Mamma patted Marcella's hand and soon coaxed her to quit sobbing.

When Dinah explained that the first she knew of Raggedy being in the wash was when she took her from the boiler, Marcella began crying again.

"It was all my fault, Mamma!" she cried. "I remember now that I threw dear old Raggedy Ann from me as I ran out the door and she must have fallen in the clothes hamper! Oh dear! Oh dear!" and she hugged Raggedy Ann tight.

Mamma did not tell Marcella that she had been cross and

naughty for she knew Marcella felt very sorry. Instead Mamma put her arms around her and said,

"Just see how Raggedy Ann takes it! She doesn't seem to be unhappy!"

And when Marcella brushed her tears away and looked at Raggedy Ann, flat as a pancake and with a cheery smile upon her painted face, she had to laugh. And Mamma and Dinah had to laugh, too, for Raggedy Ann's smile was almost twice as broad as it had been before.

"Just let me hang Miss Raggedy on the line in the bright sunshine for half an hour," said Dinah, "and you won't know her when she comes off!"

So Raggedy Ann was pinned to the clothes-line, out in the bright sunshine, where she swayed and twisted in the breeze and listened to the chatter of the robins in a nearby tree.

Every once in a while Dinah went out and rolled and patted Raggedy until her cotton stuffing was soft and dry and fluffy and her head and arms and legs were nice and round again.

Then she took Raggedy Ann into the house and showed Marcella and Mamma how clean and sweet she was.

Marcella took Raggedy Ann right up to the nursery and told all the dolls just what had happened and how sorry she was that she had been so cross and peevish when she dressed them. And while the dolls said never a word they looked at their little mistress with love in their eyes as she sat in the little red rocking chair and held Raggedy Ann tightly in her arms.

And Raggedy Ann's remaining shoe-button eye looked up at her little mistress in rather a saucy manner, but upon her face was the same old smile of happiness, good humor and love.

RAGGEDY ANN AND THE KITE

Raggedy Ann watched with interest the preparations.

A number of sticks were being fastened together with strings and covered with light cloth.

Raggedy Ann heard some of the boys talk of "The Kite," so Raggedy Ann knew this must be a kite.

When a tail had been fastened to the kite and a large ball of heavy twine tied to the front, one of the boys held the kite up in the air and another boy walked off, unwinding the ball of twine.

There was a nice breeze blowing, so the boy with the twine called, "Let 'er go" and started running.

Marcella held Raggedy up so that she could watch the kite sail through the air.

How nicely it climbed! But suddenly the kite acted strangely, and as all the children shouted advice to the boy with the ball of twine, the kite began darting this way and that, and finally making four or five loop-the-loops, it crashed to the ground.

"It needs more tail on it!" one boy shouted.

Then the children asked each other where they might get more rags to fasten to the tail of the kite.

"Let's tie Raggedy Ann to the tail!" suggested Marcella. "I know she would enjoy a trip 'way up in the sky!"

The boys all shouted with delight at this new suggestion. So Raggedy Ann was tied to the tail of the kite.

This time the kite rose straight in the air and remained steady. The boy with the ball of twine unwound it until the kite and Raggedy Ann were 'way, 'way up and far away. How Raggedy Ann enjoyed being up there! She could see for miles and miles! And how tiny the children looked!

Suddenly a great puff of wind came and carried Raggedy Ann streaming 'way out behind the kite! She could hear the wind singing on the twine as the strain increased.

Suddenly Raggedy Ann felt something rip. It was the rag to which she was tied. As each puff of wind caught her the rip widened.

When Marcella watched Raggedy Ann rise high above the field, she wondered how much Raggedy Ann enjoyed it, and wished that she, too, might have gone along. But after the kite had been up in the air for five or ten minutes, Marcella grew restless. Kites were rather tiresome. There was more fun in tea parties out under the apple tree.

"Will you please pull down the kite now?" she asked the boy with the twine. "I want Raggedy Ann."

"Let her ride up there!" the boy replied. "We'll bring her home when we pull down the kite! We're going to get another ball of twine and let her go higher!"

Marcella did not like to leave Raggedy Ann with the boys, so she sat down upon the ground to wait until they pulled down the kite.

But while Marcella watched Raggedy Ann, a dot in the sky, she could not see the wind ripping the rag to which Raggedy was tied.

Suddenly the rag parted and Raggedy Ann went sailing away as the wind caught in her skirts.

Marcella jumped from the ground, too surprised to say anything. The kite, released from the weight of Raggedy Ann began darting and swooping to the ground.

"We'll get her for you!" some of the boys said when they saw Marcella's troubled face, and they started running in the direction Raggedy Ann had fallen. Marcella and the other girls ran with them. They ran, and they ran, and they ran, and at last they found the kite upon the ground with one of the sticks broken, but they could not find Raggedy Ann anywhere.

"She must have fallen almost in your yard!" a boy said to Marcella, "for the kite was directly over here when the doll fell!"

Marcella was heartbroken. She went in the house and lay on the bed. Mamma went out with the children and tried to find Raggedy Ann, but Raggedy Ann was nowhere to be seen.

When Daddy came home in the evening he tried to find Raggedy, but met with no success. Marcella had eaten hardly any dinner, nor could she be comforted by Mamma or Daddy. The other dolls in the nursery lay forgotten and were not put to bed that night, for Marcella lay and sobbed and tossed about her bed.

Finally she said a little prayer for Raggedy Ann, and went to sleep. And as she slept Marcella dreamed that the fairies came and took Raggedy Ann with them to fairyland for a visit, and then sent Raggedy Ann home to her. She awakened with a cry. Of course Mamma came to her bed right away and said that Daddy would offer a reward in the morning for the return of Raggedy.

"It was all my fault, Mamma!" Marcella said. "I should not have offered the boys dear old Raggedy Ann to tie on the tail of the kite! But I just know the fairies will send her back."

Mamma took her in her arms and soothed her with cheering words, although she felt indeed that Raggedy Ann was truly lost and would never be found again.

Now, where do you suppose Raggedy Ann was all this time?

When Raggedy Ann dropped from the kite, the wind

caught in her skirts and carried her along until she fell in the fork of the large elm tree directly over Marcella's house. When Raggedy Ann fell with a thud, face up in the fork of the tree, two robins who had a nest near by flew chattering away.

Presently the robins returned and quarreled at Raggedy Ann for laying so close to their nest, but Raggedy Ann only smiled at them and did not move.

When the robins quieted down and quit their quarreling, one of them hopped up closer to Raggedy Ann in order to investigate.

It was Mamma Robin. She called to Daddy Robin and told him to come. "See the nice yarn! We could use it to line the nest with," she said.

So the robins hopped closer to Raggedy Ann and asked if they might have some of her yarn hair to line their nest. Raggedy Ann smiled at them. So the two robins pulled and tugged at Raggedy Ann's yarn hair until they had enough to line their nest nice and soft.

Evening came and the robins sang their good night songs, and Raggedy Ann watched the stars come out, twinkle all night and disappear in the morning light. In the morning the robins again pulled yarn from Raggedy Ann's head, and loosened her so she could peep over the side of the limb, and when the sun came up Raggedy Ann saw she was in the trees in her own yard.

Now before she could eat any breakfast, Marcella started out to find Raggedy Ann. And, it was Marcella herself who found her. And this is how she did it.

Mamma Robin had seen Marcella with Raggedy Ann out in the yard many times, so she began calling "Cheery! Cheery!" and Daddy Robin started calling "Cheery! Cheery! Cheer up! Cheer up! Cheerily Cheerily! Cheery! Cheery!" And Marcella looking up into the tree above the house to see the robins, discovered Raggedy Ann peeping over the limb at her.

Oh, how her heart beat with happiness. "Here is Raggedy Ann," she shouted.

And Mamma and Daddy came out and saw Raggedy smiling at them, and Daddy got the clothes prop and climbed out of the attic window and poked Raggedy Ann out of the tree and she fell right into Marcella's arms where she was hugged in a tight embrace.

"You'll never go up on a kite again, Raggedy Ann!" said Marcella, "for I felt so lost without you. I will never let you leave me again."

So Raggedy Ann went into the house and had breakfast with her little mistress and Mamma and Daddy smiled at each other when they peeped through the door into the breakfast room, for Raggedy Ann's smile was wide and very yellow. Marcella, her heart full of happiness, was feeding Raggedy Ann part of her egg.

RAGGEDY ANN RESCUES FIDO

It was almost midnight and the dolls were asleep in their beds; all except Raggedy Ann.

Raggedy lay there, her shoe-button eyes staring straight up at the ceiling. Every once in a while Raggedy Ann ran her rag hand up through her yarn hair. She was thinking.

When she had thought for a long, long time, Raggedy Ann raised herself on her wabbly elbows and said, "I've thought it all out."

At this the other dolls shook each other and raised up saying, "Listen! Raggedy has thought it all out!"

"Tell us what you have been thinking, dear Raggedy," said the tin soldier. "We hope they were pleasant thoughts."

"Not very pleasant thoughts!" said Raggedy, as she brushed a tear from her shoe-button eyes. "You haven't seen Fido all day, have you?"

"Not since early this morning," the French dolly said.

"It has troubled me," said Raggedy, "and if my head was not stuffed with lovely new white cotton, I am sure it would have ached with the worry! When Mistress took me into the living-room this afternoon she was crying, and I heard her mamma say, 'We will find him! He is sure to come home soon!' and I knew they were talking of Fido! He must be lost!"

The tin soldier jumped out of bed and ran over to Fido's basket, his tin feet clicking on the floor as he went. "He is not here," he said.

"When I was sitting in the window about noon-time," said the Indian doll, "I saw Fido and a yellow scraggly dog playing out on the lawn and they ran out through a hole in the fence!"

"That was Priscilla's dog, Peterkins!" said the French doll.

"I know poor Mistress is very sad on account of Fido," said the Dutch doll, "because I was in the dining-room at supper-time and I heard her daddy tell her to eat her supper and he would go out and find Fido; but I had forgotten all about it until now."

"That is the trouble with all of us except Raggedy Ann!" cried the little penny doll, in a squeaky voice, "She has to think for all of us!"

"I think it would be a good plan for us to show our love for Mistress and try and find Fido!" exclaimed Raggedy.

"It is a good plan, Raggedy Ann!" cried all the dolls. "Tell us how to start about it."

"Well, first let us go out upon the lawn and see if we can track the dogs!" said Raggedy.

"I can track them easily!" the Indian doll said, "for Indians are good at trailing things!"

"Then let us waste no more time in talking!" said Raggedy Ann, as she jumped from bed, followed by the rest.

The nursery window was open, so the dolls helped each other up on the sill and then jumped to the soft grass below. They fell in all sorts of queer attitudes, but of course the fall did not hurt them.

At the hole in the fence the Indian doll picked up the trail of the two dogs, and the dolls, stringing out behind, followed him until they came to Peterkins' house. Peterkins was surprised to see the strange little figures in white nighties come stringing up the path to the dog house.

Peterkins was too large to sleep in the nursery, so he had a nice cozy dog-house under the grape arbor.

"Come in," Peterkins said when he saw and recognized the dolls, so all the dollies went into Peterkins' house and sat about while Raggedy told him why they had come.

"It has worried me, too!" said Peterkins, "but I had no way of telling your mistress where Fido was, for she cannot understand dog language! For you see," Peterkins continued, "Fido and I were having the grandest romp over in the park when a great big man with a funny thing on the end of a stick came running towards us. We barked at him and Fido thought he was trying to play with us and went up too close and do you know, that wicked man caught Fido in the thing at the end of the stick and carried him to a wagon and dumped him in with a lot of other dogs!"

"*The Dog Catcher!*" cried Raggedy Ann.

"Yes!" said Peterkins, as he wiped his eyes with his paws. "It was the dog catcher! For I followed the wagon at a distance and I saw him put all the dogs into a big wire pen, so that none could get out!"

"Then you know the way there, Peterkins?" asked Raggedy Ann.

"Yes, I can find it easily," Peterkins said.

"Then show us the way!" Raggedy Ann cried, "for we must try to rescue Fido."

So Peterkins led the way up alleys and across streets, the dolls all pattering along behind him. It was a strange procession. Once a strange dog ran out at them, but Peterkins told him to mind his own business and the strange dog returned to his own yard.

At last they came to the dog catcher's place. Some of the dogs in the pen were barking at the moon and others were whining and crying.

There was Fido, all covered with mud, and his pretty red ribbon dragging on the ground. My, but he was glad to see the dolls and Peterkins! All the dogs came to the side of the

pen and twisted their heads from side to side, gazing in wonder at the queer figures of the dolls.

"We will try and let you out," said Raggedy Ann.

At this all the dogs barked joyfully.

Then Raggedy Ann, the other dolls and Peterkins went to the gate.

The catch was too high for Raggedy Ann to reach, but Peterkins held Raggedy Ann in his mouth and stood up on his hind legs so that she could raise the catch.

When the catch was raised, the dogs were so anxious to get out they pushed and jumped against the gate so hard it flew open, knocking Peterkins and Raggedy Ann into the mud. Such a yapping and barking was never heard in the neighborhood as when the dogs swarmed out of the enclosure, jumping over one another and scrambling about in the mad rush out the gate.

Fido picked himself up from where he had been rolled by the large dogs and helped Raggedy Ann to her feet. He, Peterkins, and all the dolls ran after the pack of dogs, turning the corner just as the dog catcher came running out of the house in his nightgown to see what was causing the trouble.

He stopped in astonishment when he saw the string of dolls in white nighties pattering down the alley, for he could not imagine what they were.

Well, you may be sure the dolls thanked Peterkins for his kind assistance and they and Fido ran on home, for a faint light was beginning to show in the east where the sun was getting ready to come up.

When they got to their own home they found an old chair out in the yard and after a great deal of work they finally dragged it to the window and thus managed to get into the nursery again.

Fido was very grateful to Raggedy Ann and the other dolls and before he went to his basket he gave them each a lick on the cheek.

The dolls lost no time in scrambling into bed and pulling up the covers, for they were very sleepy, but just as they were dozing off, Raggedy Ann raised herself and said, "If my legs and arms were not stuffed with nice clean cotton I feel sure they would ache, but being stuffed with nice clean white cotton, they do not ache and I could not feel happier if my body were stuffed with sunshine, for I know how pleased and happy Mistress will be in the morning when she discovers Fido asleep in his own little basket, safe and sound at home."

And as the dollies by this time were all asleep, Raggedy Ann pulled the sheet up to her chin and smiled so hard she ripped two stitches out of the back of her rag head.

RAGGEDY ANN AND THE PAINTER

When housecleaning time came around, Mistress' mamma decided that she would have the nursery repainted and new paper put upon the walls. That was why all the dolls happened to be laid helter-skelter upon one of the high shelves.

Mistress had been in to look at them and wished to put them to bed, but as the painters were coming again in the early morning, Mamma thought it best that their beds be piled in the closet.

So the dolls' beds were piled into the closet, one on top of another and the dolls were placed upon the high shelf.

When all was quiet that night, Raggedy Ann who was on the bottom of the pile of dolls spoke softly and asked the others if they would mind moving along the shelf.

"The cotton in my body is getting mashed as flat as a pancake!" said Raggedy Ann. And although the tin soldier was piled so that his foot was pressed into Raggedy's face, she still wore her customary smile.

So the dolls began moving off to one side until Raggedy Ann was free to sit up.

"Ah, that's a great deal better!" she said, stretching her arms and legs to get the kinks out of them, and patting her dress into shape.

"Well, I'll be glad when morning comes!" she said finally, "for I know Mistress will take us out in the yard and play with us under the trees."

So the dolls sat and talked until daylight, when the painters came to work.

One of the painters, a young fellow, seeing the dolls, reached up and took Raggedy Ann down from the shelf.

"Look at this rag doll, Jim," he said to one of the other painters, "She's a daisy," and he took Raggedy Ann by the hands and danced with her while he whistled a lively tune. Raggedy Ann's heels hit the floor thumpity-thump and she enjoyed it immensely.

The other dolls sat upon the shelf and looked straight before them, for it would never do to let grown-up men know that dolls were really alive.

"Better put her back upon the shelf," said one of the other men. "You'll have the little girl after you! The chances are that she likes that old rag doll better than any of the others!"

But the young painter twisted Raggedy Ann into funny attitudes and laughed and laughed as she looped about. Finally he got to tossing her up in the air and catching her. This was great fun for Raggedy and as she sailed up by the shelf the dolls all smiled at her, for it pleased them whenever Raggedy Ann was happy.

But the young fellow threw Raggedy Ann up into the air once too often and when she came down he failed to catch her and she came down *splash*, head first into a bucket of oily paint.

"I told you!" said the older painter, "and now you are in for it!"

"My goodness! I didn't mean to do it!" said the young fellow, "What had I better do with her?"

"Better put her back on the shelf!" replied the other.

So Raggedy was placed back upon the shelf and the paint ran from her head and trickled down upon her dress.

After breakfast, Mistress came into the nursery and saw Raggedy all covered with paint and she began crying.

The young painter felt sorry and told her how it had happened.

"If you will let me," he said, "I will take her home with me and will clean her up tonight and will bring her back day after tomorrow."

So Raggedy was wrapped in a newspaper that evening and carried away.

All the dolls felt sad that night without Raggedy Ann near them.

"Poor Raggedy! I could have cried when I saw her all covered with paint!" said the French doll.

"She didn't look like our dear old Raggedy Ann at all!" said the tin soldier, who wiped the tears from his eyes so that they would not run down on his arms and rust them.

"The paint covered her lovely smile and nose and you could not see the laughter in her shoe-button eyes!" said the Indian doll.

And so the dolls talked that night and the next. But in

the daytime when the painters were there, they kept very quiet.

The second day Raggedy was brought home and the dolls were all anxious for night to come so that they could see and talk with Raggedy Ann.

At last the painters left and the house was quiet, for Mistress had been in and placed Raggedy on the shelf with the other dolls.

"Tell us all about it, Raggedy dear!" the dolls cried.

"Oh I am so glad I fell in the paint!" cried Raggedy, after she had hugged all the dolls, "For I have had the happiest time. The painter took me home and told his Mamma how I happened to be covered with paint and she was very sorry. She took a rag and wiped off my shoe-button eyes and then I saw that she was a very pretty, sweet-faced lady and she got some cleaner and wiped off most of the paint on my face.

"But you know," Raggedy continued, "the paint had soaked through my rag head and had made the cotton inside all sticky and soggy and I could not think clearly. And my yarn hair was all matted with paint.

"So the kind lady took off my yarn hair and cut the stitches out of my head, and took out all the painty cotton.

"It was a great relief, although it felt queer at first and my thoughts seemed scattered.

"She left me in her work-basket that night and hung me out upon the clothes-line the next morning when she had washed the last of the paint off.

"And while I hung out on the clothes-line, what do you think?"

"We could never guess!" all the dolls cried.

"Why a dear little Jenny Wren came and picked enough cotton out of me to make a cute little cuddly nest in the grape arbor!"

"Wasn't that sweet!" cried all the dolls.

"Yes indeed it was!" replied Raggedy Ann, "It made me very happy. Then when the lady took me in the house again she stuffed me with lovely nice new cotton, all the way from my knees up and sewed me up and put new yarn on my head for hair and—and—and it's a secret!" said Raggedy Ann.

"Oh tell us the secret!" cried all the dolls, as they pressed closer to Raggedy. "Well, I know you will not tell anyone who would not be glad to know about it, so I will tell you the secret and why I am wearing my smile a trifle broader!" said Raggedy Ann.

The dolls all said that Raggedy Ann's smile was indeed a quarter of an inch wider on each side.

"When the dear lady put the new white cotton in my body," said Raggedy Ann "she went to the cupboard and came back with a paper bag. And she took from the bag ten or fifteen little candy hearts with mottos on them and she hunted through the candy hearts until she found a beautiful

red one which she sewed up in me with the cotton! So that is the secret, and that is why I am so happy! Feel here," said Raggedy Ann. All the dolls could feel Raggedy Ann's beautiful new candy heart and they were very happy for her.

After all had hugged each other good night and had cuddled up for the night, the tin soldier asked, "Did you have a chance to see what the motto on your new candy heart was, Raggedy Ann?"

"Oh yes," replied Raggedy Ann, "I was so happy I forgot to tell you. It had printed upon it in nice blue letters, 'I LOVE YOU.'"

RAGGEDY ANN'S TRIP ON THE RIVER

When Marcella had a tea party out in the orchard, of course all of the dolls were invited. Raggedy Ann, the tin soldier, the Indian doll and all the others—even the four little penny dolls in the spool box. After a lovely tea party with ginger cookies and milk, of course the dolls were very sleepy, at least Marcella thought so, so she took all except Raggedy Ann into the house and put them to bed for the afternoon nap. Then Marcella told Raggedy Ann to stay there and watch the things.

As there was nothing else to do, Raggedy Ann waited for Marcella to return. And as she watched the little ants eating cookie crumbs Marcella had thrown to them, she heard all of a sudden the patter of puppy feet behind her. It was Fido.

The puppy dog ran up to Raggedy Ann and twisted his head about as he looked at her. Then he put his front feet out and barked in Raggedy Ann's face. Raggedy Ann tried to look very stern, but she could not hide the broad smile painted on her face.

"Oh, you want to play, do you?" the puppy dog barked, as he jumped at Raggedy Ann and then jumped back again.

The more Raggedy Ann smiled, the livelier Fido's antics

became, until finally he caught the end of her dress and dragged her about.

This was great fun for the puppy dog, but Raggedy Ann did not enjoy it. She kicked and twisted as much as she could, but the puppy dog thought Raggedy was playing.

He ran out the garden gate and down the path across the meadow, every once in a while stopping and pretending he was very angry. When he pretended this, Fido would give Raggedy Ann a great shaking, making her yarn head hit the ground "ratty-tat-tat." Then he would give his head a toss and send Raggedy Ann high in the air where she would turn over two or three times before she reached the ground.

By this time, she had lost her apron and now some of her yarn hair was coming loose.

As Fido neared the brook, another puppy dog came running across the foot-bridge to meet him. "What have you there, Fido?" said the new puppy dog as he bounced up to Raggedy Ann.

"This is Raggedy Ann," answered Fido. "She and I are having a lovely time playing."

You see, Fido really thought Raggedy enjoyed being tossed around and whirled high up in the air. But of course she didn't. However, the game didn't last much longer. As Raggedy Ann hit the ground the new puppy dog caught her dress and ran with her across the bridge, Fido barking close behind him.

In the center of the bridge, Fido caught up with the new puppy dog and they had a lively tug-of-war with Raggedy Ann stretched between then. As they pulled and tugged and flopped Raggedy Ann about, somehow she fell over the side of the bridge into the water.

The puppy dogs were surprised, and Fido was very sorry indeed, for he remembered how good Raggedy.Ann had been to him and how she had rescued him from the dog-pound. But the current carried Raggedy Ann right along and all Fido could do was to run along the bank and bark.

Now, you would have thought Raggedy Ann would sink, but no, she floated nicely, for she was stuffed with clean white cotton and the water didn't soak through very quickly.

After a while, the strange puppy and Fido grew tired of running along the bank and the strange puppy scampered home over the meadow, with his tail carried gaily over his back as if he had nothing to be ashamed of. But Fido walked home very sorry indeed. His little heart was broken to think that he had caused Raggedy Ann to be drowned.

But Raggedy Ann didn't drown—not a bit of it. In fact, she even went to sleep on the brook, for the motion of the current was very soothing as it carried her along—just like being rocked by Marcella.

So, sleeping peacefully, Raggedy Ann drifted along with the current until she came to a pool where she lodged against a large stone.

Raggedy Ann tried to climb upon the stone, but by this time the water had thoroughly soaked through Raggedy Ann's nice, clean, white cotton stuffing and she was so heavy she could not climb.

So there she had to stay until Marcella and Daddy came along and found her.

You see, they had been looking for her. They had found pieces of her apron all along the path and across the meadow where Fido and the strange puppy dog had shaken them from Raggedy Ann. So they followed the brook until they found her.

When Daddy fished Raggedy Ann from the water, Marcella hugged her so tightly to her breast the water ran from Raggedy Ann and dripped all over Marcella's apron. But Marcella was so glad to find Raggedy Ann again she didn't mind it a bit. She just hurried home and took off all of Raggedy Ann's wet clothes and placed her on a little red chair in front of the oven door, and then brought all of the other dolls in and read a fairy tale to them while Raggedy Ann steamed and dried.

When Raggedy Ann was thoroughly dry, Mamma said she thought the cake must be finished and she took from the oven a lovely chocolate cake and gave Marcella a large piece to have another tea party with.

That night when all the house was asleep, Raggedy Ann raised up in bed and said to the dolls who were still awake, "I am so happy I do not feel a bit sleepy. Do you know, I believe the water soaked me so thoroughly my candy heart must have melted and filled my whole body, and I do not feel the least bit angry with Fido for playing with me so roughly!"

So all the other dolls were happy, too, for happiness is very easy to catch when we love one another and are sweet all through.

RAGGEDY ANN AND THE STRANGE DOLLS

Raggedy Ann lay just as Marcella had dropped her—all sprawled out with her rag arms and legs twisted in ungraceful attitudes.

Her yarn hair was twisted and lay partly over her face, hiding one of her shoe-button eyes.

Raggedy gave no sign that she had heard, but lay there smiling at the ceiling.

Perhaps Raggedy Ann knew that what the new dolls said was true.

But sometimes the truth may hurt and this may have been the reason Raggedy Ann lay there so still.

"Did you ever see such an ungainly creature!"

"I do believe it has shoe buttons for eyes!"

"And yarn hair!"

"Mercy, did you ever see such feet!"

The Dutch doll rolled off the doll sofa and said "Mamma" in his quavery voice, he was so surprised at hearing anyone speak so of beloved Raggedy Ann—dear Raggedy Ann, she of the candy heart, whom all the dolls loved.

Uncle Clem was also very much surprised and offended. He walked up in front of the two new dolls and looked them sternly in the eyes, but he could think of nothing to say so he pulled at his yarn mustache.

Marcella had only received the two new dolls that morning. They had come in the morning mail and were presents from an aunt.

Marcella had named the two new dolls Annabel-Lee and Thomas, after her aunt and uncle.

Annabel-Lee and Thomas were beautiful dolls and must have cost heaps and heaps of shiny pennies, for both were handsomely dressed and had *real* hair!

Annabel's hair was of a lovely shade of auburn and Thomas' was golden yellow.

Annabel was dressed in soft, lace-covered silk and upon her head she wore a beautiful hat with long silk ribbons tied in a neat bow-knot beneath her dimpled chin.

Thomas was dressed in an Oliver Twist suit of dark velvet with a lace collar. Both he and Annabel wore lovely black slippers and short stockings.

They were sitting upon two of the little red doll chairs where Marcella had placed them and where they could see the other dolls.

When Uncle Clem walked in front of them and pulled his mustache they laughed outright. "Tee-Hee-Hee!" they snickered, "He has holes in his knees!"

Quite true. Uncle Clem was made of worsted and the moths had eaten his knees and part of his kiltie. He had a kiltie, you see, for Uncle Clem was a Scotch doll.

Uncle Clem shook, but he felt so hurt he could think of nothing to say.

He walked over and sat down beside Raggedy Ann and brushed her yarn hair away from her shoe-button eye.

The tin soldier went over and sat beside them.

"Don't you mind what they say, Raggedy!" he said, "They do not know you as we do!"

"We don't care to know her!" said Annabel-Lee as she primped her dress, "She looks like a scarecrow!"

"And the Soldier must have been made with a can opener!" laughed Thomas.

"You should be ashamed of yourselves!" said the French dolly, as she stood before Annabel and Thomas, "You will make all of us sorry that you have joined our family if you continue to poke fun at us and look down upon us. We are all happy here together and share in each others' adventures and happiness."

Now, that night Marcella did not undress the two new dolls, for she had no nighties for them, so she let them sit up in the two little red doll chairs so they would not muss their clothes. "I will make nighties for you tomorrow!" she said as she kissed them good night. Then she went over and gave Raggedy Ann a good night hug. "Take good care of all my children, Raggedy!" she said as she went out.

Annabel and Thomas whispered together, "Perhaps we have been too hasty in our judgment!" said Annabel-Lee. "This Raggedy Ann seems to be a favorite with the mistress and with all the dolls!"

"There must be a reason!" replied Thomas, "I am beginning to feel sorry that we spoke of her looks. One really cannot help one's looks after all."

Now, Annabel-Lee and Thomas were very tired after their long journey and soon they fell asleep and forgot all about the other dolls.

When they were sound asleep, Raggedy Ann slipped quietly from her bed and awakened the tin soldier and Uncle Clem and the three tiptoed to the two beautiful new dolls.

They lifted them gently so as not to awaken them and carried them to Raggedy Ann's bed.

Raggedy Ann tucked them in snugly and lay down upon the hard floor.

The tin soldier and Uncle Clem both tried to coax Raggedy Ann into accepting their bed (they slept together), but Raggedy Ann would not hear of it.

"I am stuffed with nice soft cotton and the hard floor does not bother me at all!" said Raggedy.

At daybreak the next morning Annabel and Thomas awak-

ened to find themselves in Raggedy Ann's bed and as they raised up and looked at each other each knew how ashamed the other felt, for they knew Raggedy Ann had generously given them her bed.

There Raggedy Ann lay; all sprawled out upon the hard floor, her rag arms and legs twisted in ungraceful attitudes.

"How good and honest she looks!" said Annabel. "It must be her shoe-button eyes!"

"How nicely her yarn hair falls in loops over her face!" exclaimed Thomas, "I did not notice how pleasant her face looked last night!"

"The others seem to love her ever and ever so much!" mused Annabel. "It must be because she is so kind."

Both new dolls were silent for a while, thinking deeply.

"How do you feel?" Thomas finally asked.

"Very much ashamed of myself!" answered Annabel, "And you, Thomas?"

"As soon as Raggedy Ann awakens, I shall tell her just how much ashamed I am of myself and if she can, I want her to forgive me!" Thomas said.

"The more I look at her, the better I like her!" said Annabel.

"I am going to kiss her!" said Thomas.

"You'll awaken her if you do!" said Annabel.

But Thomas climbed out of bed and kissed Raggedy Ann on her painted cheek and smoothed her yarn hair from her rag forehead.

And Annabel-Lee climbed out of bed, too, and kissed Raggedy Ann.

Then Thomas and Annabel-Lee gently carried Raggedy Ann and put her in her own bed and tenderly tucked her in, and then took their seats in the two little red chairs.

After a while Annabel said softly to Thomas, "I feel ever and ever so much better and happier!"

"So do I!" Thomas replied. "It's like a whole lot of

sunshine coming into a dark room, and I shall always try to keep it there!"

Fido had one fuzzy white ear sticking up over the edge of his basket and he gave his tail a few thumps against his pillow.

Raggedy Ann lay quietly in bed where Thomas and Annabel had tucked her. And as she smiled at the ceiling, her candy heart (with "I LOVE YOU" written on it) thrilled with contentment, for, as you have probably guessed, Raggedy Ann had not been asleep at all!

RAGGEDY ANN AND THE KITTENS

Raggedy Ann had been away all day.

Marcella had come early in the morning and dressed all the dolls and placed them about the nursery.

Some of the dolls had been put in the little red chairs around the little doll table. There was nothing to eat upon the table except a turkey, a fried egg and an apple, all made of plaster of paris and painted in natural colors. The little teapot and other doll dishes were empty, but Marcella had told them to enjoy their dinner while she was away.

The French dolly had been given a seat upon the doll sofa and Uncle Clem had been placed at the piano.

Marcella picked up Raggedy Ann and carried her out of the nursery when she left, telling the dolls to "be real good children, while Mamma is away!"

When the door closed, the tin soldier winked at the Dutch-boy doll and handed the imitation turkey to the penny dolls. "Have some nice turkey?" he asked.

"No thank you!" the penny dolls said in little penny-doll, squeaky voices, "We have had all we can eat!"

"Shall I play you a tune?" asked Uncle Clem of the French doll.

At this all the dolls laughed, for Uncle Clem could not begin to play any tune. Raggedy Ann was the only doll who had ever taken lessons, and she could play Peter-Peter-Pumpkin-Eater with one hand.

In fact, Marcella had almost worn out Raggedy Ann's right hand teaching it to her.

"Play something lively!" said the French doll, as she giggled behind her hand, so Uncle Clem began hammering the eight keys on the toy piano with all his might until a noise was heard upon the stairs.

Quick as a wink, all the dolls took the same positions in which they had been placed by Marcella, for they did not wish really truly people to know that they could move about.

But it was only Fido. He put his nose in the door and looked around.

All the dolls at the table looked steadily at the painted food, and Uncle Clem leaned upon the piano keys looking just as unconcerned as when he had been placed there.

Then Fido pushed the door open and came into the nursery wagging his tail.

He walked over to the table and sniffed, in hopes Marcella had given the dolls real food and that some would still be left.

"Where's Raggedy Ann?" Fido asked, when he had satisfied himself that there was no food.

"Mistress took Raggedy Ann and went somewhere!" all the dolls answered in chorus.

"I've found something I must tell Raggedy Ann about!" said Fido, as he scratched his ear.

"Is it a secret?" asked the penny dolls.

"Secret nothing," replied Fido, "It's kittens!"

"How lovely!" cried all the dolls, "Really live kittens?"

"Really live kittens!" replied Fido, "Three little tiny ones, out in the barn!"

"Oh, I wish Raggedy Ann was here!" cried the French doll. "She would know what to do about it!"

"That's why I wanted to see her," said Fido, as he thumped his tail on the floor, "I did not know there were any

kittens and I went into the barn to hunt for mice and the first thing I knew Mamma Cat came bouncing right at me with her eyes looking green! I tell you I hurried out of there!"

"How did you know there were any kittens then?" asked Uncle Clem.

"I waited around the barn until Mamma Cat went up to the house and then I slipped into the barn again, for I knew there must be something inside or she would not have jumped at me that way! We are always very friendly, you know." Fido continued. "And what was my surprise to find three tiny little kittens in an old basket, 'way back in a dark corner!"

"Go get them, Fido, and bring them up so we can see them!" said the tin soldier.

"Not me!" said Fido, "If I had a suit of tin clothes on like you have I might do it, but you know cats can scratch very hard if they want to!"

"We will tell Raggedy when she comes in!" said the French doll, and then Fido went out to play with a neighbor dog.

So when Raggedy Ann had been returned to the nursery the dolls could hardly wait until Marcella had put on their nighties and left them for the night.

Then they told Raggedy Ann all about the kittens.

Raggedy Ann jumped from her bed and ran over to Fido's basket; he wasn't there.

Then Raggedy suggested that all the dolls go out to the barn and see the kittens. This they did easily, for the window was open and it was but a short jump to the ground.

They found Fido out near the barn watching a hole.

"I was afraid something might disturb them," he said, "for Mamma Cat went away about an hour ago."

All the dolls, with Raggedy Ann in the lead, crawled through the hole and ran to the basket.

Just as Raggedy Ann started to pick up one of the kittens

there was a lot of howling and yelping and Fido came bounding through the hole with Mamma Cat behind him. When Mamma Cat caught up with Fido he would yelp.

When Fido and Mamma Cat had circled the barn two or three times Fido managed to find the hole and escape to the yard; then Mamma Cat came over to the basket and saw all the dolls.

"I'm s'prised at you, Mamma Cat!" said Raggedy Ann, "Fido has been watching your kittens for an hour while you were away. He wouldn't hurt them for anything!"

"I'm sorry, then," said Mamma Cat.

"You must trust Fido, Mamma Cat!" said Raggedy Ann, "because he loves you and anyone who loves you can be trusted!"

"That's so!" replied Mamma Cat. "Cats love mice, too, and I wish the mice trusted us more!"

The dolls all laughed at this joke.

"Have you told the folks up at the house about your dear little kittens?" Raggedy Ann asked.

"Oh, my, no!" exclaimed Mamma Cat. "At the last place I lived the people found out about my kittens and do you know, all the kittens disappeared! I intend keeping this a secret!"

"But all the folks at this house are very kindly people and would dearly love your kittens!" cried all the dolls.

"Let's take them right up to the nursery!" said Raggedy Ann, "And Mistress can find them there in the morning!"

"How lovely!" said all the dolls in chorus. "Do, Mamma Cat! Raggedy Ann knows, for she is stuffed with nice clean white cotton and is very wise!"

So after a great deal of persuasion, Mamma Cat finally consented. Raggedy Ann took two of the kittens and carried them to the house while Mamma Cat carried the other.

Raggedy Ann wanted to give the kittens her bed, but Fido, who was anxious to prove his affection, insisted that Mamma Cat and the kittens should have his nice soft basket.

The dolls could hardly sleep that night; they were so anxious to see what Mistress would say when she found the dear little kittens in the morning.

Raggedy Ann did not sleep a wink, for she shared her bed with Fido and he kept her awake whispering to her.

In the morning when Marcella came to the nursery, the first thing she saw was the three little kittens.

She cried out in delight and carried them all down to show to Mamma and Daddy. Mamma Cat went trailing along, arching her back and purring with pride as she rubbed against all the chairs and doors.

Mamma and Daddy said the kittens could stay in the nursery and belong to Marcella, so Marcella took them back to Fido's basket while she hunted names for them out of a fairy tale book.

Marcella finally decided upon three names; Prince Charming for the white kitty, Cinderella for the Maltese and Princess Golden for the kitty with the yellow stripes.

So that is how the three little kittens came to live in the nursery.

And it all turned out just as Raggedy Ann had said, for her head was stuffed with clean white cotton, and she could think exceedingly wise thoughts.

And Mamma Cat found out that Fido was a very good friend, too. She grew to trust him so much she would even let him help wash the kittens' faces.

RAGGEDY ANN AND THE FAIRIES' GIFT

All the dolls were tucked snugly in their little doll-beds for the night and the large house was very still.

Every once in a while Fido would raise one ear and partly open one eye, for his keen dog sense seemed to tell him that something was about to happen.

Finally he opened both eyes, sniffed into the air and, getting out of his basket and shaking himself, he trotted across the nursery to Raggedy Ann's bed.

Fido put his cold nose in Raggedy Ann's neck. She raised her head from the little pillow.

"Oh! It's you, Fido!" said Raggedy Ann. "I dreamed the tin soldier put an icicle down my neck!"

"I can't sleep," Fido told Raggedy Ann. "I feel that something is about to happen!"

"You have been eating too many bones lately, Fido, and they keep you awake," Raggedy replied.

"No, it isn't that. I haven't had any bones since the folks had beef last Sunday. It isn't that. Listen, Raggedy!"

Raggedy Ann listened.

There was a murmur as if someone were singing, far away.

"What is it?" asked Fido.

"Sh!" cautioned Raggedy Ann, "It's music."

It was indeed music, the most beautiful music Raggedy Ann had ever heard.

It grew louder, but still seemed to be *far* away.

Raggedy Ann and Fido could hear it distinctly and it sounded as if hundreds of voices were singing in unison.

"Please don't howl, Fido," Raggedy Ann said as she put her two rag arms around the dog's nose. Fido usually "sang" when he heard music.

But Fido did not sing this time; he was filled with wonder. It seemed as if something very nice was going to happen.

Raggedy Ann sat upright in bed. The room was flooded with a strange, beautiful light and the music came floating in through the nursery window.

Raggedy Ann hopped from her bed and ran across the floor, trailing the bed clothes behind her. Fido followed close behind and together they looked out the window across the flower garden.

There among the flowers were hundreds of tiny beings, some playing on tiny reed instruments and flower horns, while others sang. This was the strange, wonderful music Raggedy and Fido had heard.

"It's the Fairies!" said Raggedy Ann. "To your basket quick, Fido! They are coming this way!" And Raggedy Ann ran back to her bed, with the bed clothes trailing behind her.

Fido gave three jumps and he was in his basket, pretending he was sound asleep, but one little black eye was peeping through a chink in the side.

Raggedy jumped into her bed and pulled the covers to her chin, but lay so that her shoe-button eyes could see towards the window.

Little Fairy forms radiant as silver came flitting into the nursery, singing in far away voices. They carried a little bundle. A beautiful light came from this bundle, and to Raggedy Ann and Fido it seemed like sunshine and moon-

JOHNNY GRUELLE

shine mixed.   It was a soft mellow light, just the sort of light
you would expect to accompany Fairy Folk.

As Raggedy watched, her candy heart went pitty-pat
against her cotton stuffing, for she saw a tiny pink foot
sticking out of the bundle of light.

The Fairy troop sailed across the nursery and through the
door with their bundle and Raggedy Ann and Fido listened to
their far away music as they went down the hall.

Presently the Fairies returned without the bundle and
disappeared through the nursery window.

Raggedy Ann and Fido again ran to the window and saw
the Fairy troop dancing among the flowers.

The light from the bundle still hung about the nursery
and a strange lovely perfume floated about.

When the Fairies' music ceased and they had flown away,
Raggedy Ann and Fido returned to Raggedy's bed to think it
all out.

When old Mister Sun peeped over the garden wall and
into the nursery, and the other dolls awakened, Raggedy Ann
and Fido were still puzzled.

"What is it, Raggedy Ann?" asked the tin soldier and Uncle Clem, in one voice.

Before Raggedy Ann could answer, Marcella came running into the nursery, gathered up all the dolls in her arms, and ran down the hall, Fido jumping beside her and barking shrilly.

"Be quiet!" Marcella said to Fido, "It's asleep and you might awaken it!"

Mamma helped Marcella arrange all the dolls in a circle around the bed so that they could all see what was in the bundle.

Mamma gently pulled back the soft covering and the dolls saw a tiny little fist as pink as coral, a soft little face with a cunning tiny pink nose, and a little head as bald as the French dolly's when her hair came off.

My, how the dollies all chattered when they were once again left alone in the nursery!

"A dear cuddly baby brother for Mistress!" said Uncle Clem.

"A beautiful bundle of love and Fairy Sunshine for everybody in the house!" said Raggedy Ann, as she went to the toy piano and joyously played "Peter-Peter-Pumpkin-Eater" with one rag hand.

RAGGEDY ANN AND THE CHICKENS

When Marcella was called into the house she left Raggedy sitting on the chicken yard fence. "Now you sit quietly and do not stir," Marcella told Raggedy Ann, "If you move you may fall and hurt yourself!"

So, Raggedy Ann sat quietly, just as Marcella told her, but she smiled at the chickens for she had fallen time and again and it had never hurt her in the least. She was stuffed with nice soft cotton, you see.

So, there she sat until a tiny little humming-bird, in search of flower honey hummed close to Raggedy Ann's head and hovered near the tall Hollyhocks.

Raggedy Ann turned her rag head to see the humming-bird and lost her balance—*plump!* she went, down amongst the chickens.

The chickens scattered in all directions, all except Old Ironsides, the rooster.

He ruffled his neck feathers and put his head down close to the ground, making a queer whistling noise as he looked fiercely at Raggedy Ann.

But Raggedy Ann only smiled at Old Ironsides, the rooster, and ran her rag hand through her yarn hair for she did not fear him.

And then something strange happened, for when she made

this motion the old rooster jumped up in the air and kicked his feet out in front, knocking Raggedy Ann over and over.

When Raggedy Ann stopped rolling she waved her apron at the rooster and cried, "Shoo!" but instead of "shooing," Old Ironsides upset her again.

Now, two old hens who had been watching the rooster jump at Raggedy ran up and as one old hen placed herself before the rooster, the other old hen caught hold of Raggedy's apron and dragged her into the chicken-coop.

It was dark inside and Raggedy could not tell what was going on as she felt herself being pulled up over the nests.

But, finally Raggedy could sit up, for the old hen had quit pulling her, and as her shoe-button eyes were very good, she soon made out the shape of the old hen in front of her.

"My! that's the hardest work I have done in a long time!" said the old hen, when she could catch her breath. "I was afraid Mr. Rooster would tear your dress and apron!"

"That was a queer game he was playing, Mrs. Hen," said Raggedy Ann.

The old hen chuckled 'way down in her throat, "Gracious me! He wasn't playing a game, he was fighting you!"

"Fighting!" cried Raggedy Ann in surprise.

"Oh yes, indeed!" the old hen answered, "Old Ironsides, the rooster, thought you intended to harm some of the children chickens and he was fighting you!"

"I am sorry that I fell inside the pen, I wouldn't harm anything," Raggedy Ann said.

"If we tell you a secret you must promise not to tell your mistress!" said the old hens.

"I promise! Cross my candy heart!" said Raggedy Ann.

Then the two old hens took Raggedy Ann 'way back in the farthest corner of the chicken coop. There, in back of a box, they had built two nests and each old hen had ten eggs in her nest.

"If your folks hear of it they will take the eggs!" said the hens, "and then we could not raise our families!"

Raggedy Ann felt the eggs and they were nice and warm.

"We just left the nests when you fell into the pen!" explained the old hens.

"But how can the eggs grow if you sit upon them?" said Raggedy. "If Fido sits on any of the garden, the plants will not grow, Mistress says!"

"Eggs are different!" one old hen explained. "In order to make the eggs hatch properly, we must sit on them three weeks and not let them get cold at any time!"

"And at the end of the three weeks do the eggs sprout?" asked Raggedy Ann.

"You must be thinking of eggplant!" cried one old hen. "These eggs hatch at the end of three weeks—they don't sprout—and then we have a lovely family of soft downy chickies; little puff balls that we can cuddle under our wings and love dearly!"

"Have you been sitting upon the eggs very long?" Raggedy asked.

"Neither one of us has kept track of the time," said one hen. "So we do not know! You see, we never leave the nests only just once in a while to get a drink and to eat a little.

So we can hardly tell when it is day and when it is night."

"We were going out to get a drink when you fell in the pen!" said one old hen. "Now we will have to sit upon the eggs and warm them up again!"

The two old hens spread their feathers and nestled down upon the nests.

"When you get them good and warm, I would be glad to sit upon the eggs to keep them warm until you get something to eat and drink!" said Raggedy. So the two old hens walked out of the coop to finish their meal which had been interrupted by Raggedy's fall and while they were gone, Raggedy Ann sat quietly upon the warm eggs. Suddenly down beneath her she heard something go, "Pick, pick!" "I hope it isn't a mouse!" Raggedy Ann said to herself, when she felt something move. "I wish the old hens would come back." But when they came back and saw the puzzled expression on her face, they cried, "What is it?"

Raggedy Ann got to her feet and looked down and there were several little fluffy, cuddly baby chickies, round as little puff-balls.

"Cheep! Cheep! Cheep!" they cried when Raggedy stepped out of the nest.

"Baby Chicks!" Raggedy cried, as she stooped and picked up one of the little puff-balls. "They want to be cuddled!"

The two old hens, their eyes shining with happiness, got upon the nests and spread out their soft warm feathers, "The other eggs will hatch soon!" said they.

So, for several days Raggedy helped the two hens hatch out the rest of the chickies and just as they finished, Marcella came inside looking around.

"How in the world did you get in here, Raggedy Ann?" she cried. "I have been looking all about for you! Did the chickens drag you in here?"

Both old hens down behind the box clucked softly to the chickies beneath them and Marcella overheard them.

She lifted the box away and gave a little squeal of surprise and happiness.

"Oh you dear old Hennypennies!" she cried, lifting both old hens from their nests. "You have hidden your nests away back here and now you have one, two, three, four—twenty chickies!" and as she counted them, Marcella placed them in her apron; then catching up Raggedy Ann, she placed her over the new little chickies.

"Come on, old Hennypennies!" she said, and went out of the coop with the two old hens clucking at her heels.

Marcella called Daddy and Daddy rolled two barrels out under one of the trees and made a nice bed in each. Then he nailed slats across the front, leaving a place for a door. Each Hennypennie was then given ten little chickies and shut up in the barrel. And all the dolls were happy when they heard of Raggedy's adventure and they did not have to wait long before they were all taken out to see the new chickies.

RAGGEDY ANN AND THE MOUSE

Jeanette was a new wax doll, and like Henny, the Dutch doll, she could say "Mamma" when anyone tipped her backward or forward. She had lovely golden brown curls of real hair. It could be combed and braided, or curled or fluffed without tangling, and Raggedy Ann was very proud when Jeanette came to live with the dolls.

But now Raggedy Ann was very angry—in fact, Raggedy Ann had just ripped two stitches out of the top of her head when she took her rag hands and pulled her rag face down into a frown (but when she let go of the frown her face stretched right back into her usual cheery smile).

And *you* would have been angry, too, for something had happened to Jeanette.

Something or someone had stolen into the nursery that night when the dolls were asleep and nibbled all the wax from Jeanette's beautiful face—and now all her beauty was gone!

"It really is a shame!" said Raggedy Ann as she put her arms about Jeanette.

"Something must be done about it!" said the French doll as she stamped her little foot.

"If I catch the culprit, I will—well, I don't know what I will do with him!" said the tin soldier, who could be very fierce at times, although he was seldom cross.

"Here is the hole he came from!" cried Uncle Clem from the other end of the nursery. "Come, see!"

All the dolls ran to where Uncle Clem was, down on his hands and knees.

"This must be the place!" said Raggedy Ann. "We will plug up the hole with something, so he will not come out again!"

The dolls hunted around and brought rags and pieces of paper and pushed them into the mouse's doorway.

"I thought I heard nibbling last night," one of the penny dolls said. "You know I begged for an extra piece of pie last evening, when Mistress had me at the table and it kept me awake!"

While the dolls were talking, Marcella ran down-stairs with Jeanette and told Daddy and Mamma, who came up-stairs with Marcella and hunted around until they discovered the mouse's doorway.

"Oh, why couldn't it have chewed on me?" Raggedy Ann asked herself when she saw Marcella's sorrowful face, for Raggedy Ann was never selfish.

"Daddy will take Jeanette down-town with him and have her fixed up as good as new," said Mamma, so Jeanette was wrapped in soft tissue paper and taken away.

Later in the day Marcella came bouncing into the nursery with a surprise for the dolls. It was a dear fuzzy little kitten.

Marcella introduced the kitten to all the dolls.

"Her name is Boots, because she has four little white feet!" said Marcella. So Boots, the happy little creature, played with the penny dolls, scraping them over the floor and peeping out from behind chairs and pouncing upon them as if they were mice and the penny dolls enjoyed it hugely.

When Marcella was not in the nursery, Raggedy Ann wrestled with Boots and they would roll over and over upon the floor, Boots with her front feet around Raggedy Ann's neck and kicking with her hind feet.

JOHNNY GRUELLE

Then Boots would arch her back and pretend she was very angry and walk sideways until she was close to Raggedy. Then she would jump at her and over and over they would roll, their heads hitting the floor bumpity-bump.

Boots slept in the nursery that night and was lonely for her Mamma, for it was the first time she had been away from home.

Even though her bed was right on top of Raggedy Ann, she could not sleep. But Raggedy Ann was very glad to have Boots sleep with her, even if she was heavy, and when Boots began crying for her Mamma, Raggedy Ann comforted her and soon Boots went to sleep.

One day Jeanette came home. She had a new coating of wax on her face and she was as beautiful as ever.

Now, by this time Boots was one of the family and did not cry at night. Besides Boots was told of the mouse in the corner and how he had eaten Jeanette's wax, so she promised to sleep with one eye open.

Late that night when Boots was the only one awake, out popped a tiny mouse from the hole. Boots jumped after the mouse, and hit against the toy piano and made the keys tinkle so loudly it awakened the dolls.

They ran over to where Boots sat growling with the tiny mouse in her mouth.

My! how the mouse was squeaking!

Raggedy Ann did not like to hear it squeak, but she did not wish Jeanette to have her wax face chewed again, either.

So, Raggedy Ann said to the tiny little mouse, "You should have known better than to come here when Boots is with us. Why don't you go out in the barn and live where you will not destroy anything of value?"

"I did not know!" squeaked the little mouse, "This is the first time I have ever been here!"

"Aren't you the little mouse who nibbled Jeanette's wax face?" Raggedy Ann asked.

"No!" the little mouse answered. "I was visiting the mice inside the walls and wandered out here to pick up cake crumbs! I have three little baby mice at home down in the barn. I have never nibbled at anyone's wax face!"

"Are you a Mamma mouse?" Uncle Clem asked.

"Yes!" the little mouse squeaked, "and if the kitten will let me go I will run right home to my children and never return again!"

"Let her go, Boots!" the dolls all cried, "She has three little baby mice at home! Please let her go!"

"No, sir!" Boots growled, "This is the first mouse I have ever caught and I will eat her!" At this the little Mamma mouse began squeaking louder than ever.

"If you do not let the Mamma mouse go, Boots, I shall not play with you again!" said Raggedy Ann.

"Raggedy will not play with Boots again!" said all of the dolls in an awed tone. Not to have Raggedy play with them would have been sad, indeed.

But Boots only growled.

The dolls drew to one side, where Raggedy Ann and Uncle Clem whispered together.

And while they whispered Boots would let the little Mamma mouse run a piece, then she would catch it again and box it about between her paws.

This she did until the poor little Mamma mouse grew so tired it could scarcely run away from Boots.

Boots would let it get almost to the hole in the wall before she would catch it, for she knew it would not escape her.

As she watched the little mouse crawling towards the hole scarcely able to move, Raggedy Ann could not keep the tears from her shoe-button eyes.

Finally as Boots started to spring after the little mouse again, Raggedy Ann threw her rag arms around the kitten's neck. "Run, Mamma mouse!" Raggedy Ann cried, as Boots whirled her over and over.

Uncle Clem ran and pushed the Mamma mouse into the hole and then she was gone.

When Raggedy Ann took her arms from around Boots, the kitten was very angry. She laid her ears back and scratched Raggedy Ann with her claws.

But Raggedy Ann only smiled—it did not hurt her a bit for Raggedy was sewed together with a needle and thread and if that did not hurt, how could the scratch of a kitten? Finally Boots felt ashamed of herself and went over and lay down by the hole in the wall in hopes the mouse would return, but the mouse never returned. Even then Mamma mouse was out in the barn with her children, warning them to beware of kittens and cats.

Raggedy Ann and all the dolls then went to bed and Raggedy had just dozed off to sleep when she felt something jump upon her bed. It was Boots. She felt a warm little pink tongue caress her rag cheek. Raggedy Ann smiled happily to herself, for Boots had curled up on top of Raggedy Ann and was purring herself to sleep.

Then Raggedy Ann knew she had been forgiven for rescuing the Mamma mouse and she smiled herself to sleep and dreamed happily of tomorrow.

RAGGEDY ANN'S NEW SISTERS

Marcella was having a tea party up in the nursery when Daddy called to her, so she left the dollies sitting around the tiny table and ran down stairs carrying Raggedy Ann with her.

Mama, Daddy and a strange man were talking in the living room and Daddy introduced Marcella to the stranger.

The stranger was a large man with kindly eyes and a cheery smile, as pleasant as Raggedy Ann's.

He took Marcella upon his knee and ran his fingers through her curls as he talked to Daddy and Mamma, so, of course, Raggedy Ann liked him from the beginning. "I have two little girls," he told Marcella. "Their names are Virginia and Doris, and one time when we were at the sea-shore they were playing in the sand and they covered up Freddy, Doris' boy-doll in the sand. They were playing that Freddy was in bathing and that he wanted to be covered with the clean white sand, just as the other bathers did. And when they had covered Freddy they took their little pails and shovels and went farther down the beach to play and forgot all about Freddy.

"Now when it came time for us to go home, Virginia and Doris remembered Freddy and ran down to get him, but the tide had come in and Freddy was 'way out under the water and they could not find him. Virginia and Doris were very sad and they talked of Freddy all the way home."

"It was too bad they forgot Freddy," said Marcella.

"Yes, indeed it was!" the new friend replied as he took Raggedy Ann up and made her dance on Marcella's knee. "But it turned out all right after all, for do you know what happened to Freddy?"

"No, what did happen to him?" Marcella asked.

"Well, first of all, when Freddy was covered with the sand, he enjoyed it immensely. And he did not mind it so much when the tide came up over him, for he felt Virginia and Doris would return and get him.

"But presently Freddy felt the sand above him move as if someone was digging him out. Soon his head was uncovered and he could look right up through the pretty green water, and what do you think was happening? The Tide Fairies were uncovering Freddy!

"When he was completely uncovered, the Tide Fairies swam with Freddy 'way out to the Undertow Fairies. The Undertow Fairies took Freddy and swam with him 'way out to the Roller Fairies. The Roller Fairies carried Freddy up to the surface and tossed him up to the Spray Fairies who carried him to the Wind Fairies."

"And the Wind Fairies?" Marcella asked breathlessly.

"The Wind Fairies carried Freddy right to our garden and there Virginia and Doris found him, none the worse for his wonderful adventure!"

"Freddy must have enjoyed it and your little girls must have been very glad to get Freddy back again!" said Marcella. "Raggedy Ann went up in the air on the tail of a kite one day and fell and was lost, so now I am very careful with her!"

"Would you let me take Raggedy Ann for a few days?" asked the new friend.

Marcella was silent. She liked the stranger friend, but she did not wish to lose Raggedy Ann.

"I will promise to take very good care of her and return her to you in a week. Will you let her go with me, Marcella?"

Marcella finally agreed and when the stranger friend left, he placed Raggedy Ann in his grip.

"It is lonely without Raggedy Ann!" said the dollies each night.

"We miss her happy painted smile and her cheery ways!" they said.

And so the week dragged by. . . . .

But, my! What a chatter there was in the nursery the first night after Raggedy Ann returned. All the dolls were so anxious to hug Raggedy Ann they could scarcely wait until Marcella had left them alone.

When they had squeezed Raggedy Ann almost out of shape and she had smoothed out her yarn hair, patted her apron out and felt her shoe-button eyes to see if they were still there, she said, "Well, what have you been doing? Tell me all the news!"

"Oh we have just had the usual tea parties and games!" said the tin soldier. "Tell us about yourself, Raggedy dear, we have missed you so much!"

"Yes! Tell us where you have been and what you have done, Raggedy!" all the dolls cried.

But Raggedy Ann just then noticed that one of the penny dolls had a hand missing.

"How did this happen?" she asked as she picked up the doll.

"I fell off the table and lit upon the tin soldier last night when we were playing. But don't mind a little thing like that, Raggedy Ann," replied the penny doll. "Tell us of yourself! Have you had a nice time?"

"I shall not tell a thing until your hand is mended!" Raggedy Ann said.

So the Indian ran and brought a bottle of glue. "Where's the hand?" Raggedy asked.

"In my pocket," the penny doll answered.

When Raggedy Ann had glued the penny doll's hand in place and wrapped a rag around it to hold it until the glue dried, she said, "When I tell you of this wonderful adventure, I know you will all feel very happy. It has made me almost burst my stitches with joy."

The dolls all sat upon the floor around Raggedy Ann, the tin soldier with his arm over her shoulder.

"Well, first when I left," said Raggedy Ann, "I was placed in the Stranger Friend's grip. It was rather stuffy in there, but I did not mind it; in fact I believe I must have fallen asleep, for when I awakened I saw the Stranger Friend's hand reaching into the grip. Then he lifted me from the grip and danced me upon his knee. 'What do you think of her?' he asked to three other men sitting nearby.

"I was so interested in looking out of the window I did not pay any attention to what they said, for we were on a train and the scenery was just flying by! Then I was put back in the grip.

"When next I was taken from the grip I was in a large, clean, light room and there were many, many girls all dressed in white aprons.

"The stranger friend showed me to another man and to the girls who took off my clothes, cut my seams and took out my cotton. And what do you think! They found my lovely candy heart had not melted at all as I thought. Then they laid me on a table and marked all around my outside edges with a pencil on clean white cloth, and then the girls re-stuffed me and dressed me.

"I stayed in the clean big light room for two or three days and nights and watched my Sisters grow from pieces of cloth into rag dolls just like myself!"

"Your SISTERS!" the dolls all exclaimed in astonishment, "What do you mean, Raggedy?"

"I mean," said Raggedy Ann, "that the Stranger Friend had borrowed me from Marcella so that he could have patterns made from me. And before I left the big clean white room there where hundreds of rag dolls so like me you would not have been able to tell us apart."

"We could have told *you* by your happy smile!" cried the French dolly.

"But all of my sister dolls have smiles just like mine!" replied Raggedy Ann.

"And shoe-button eyes?" the dolls all asked.

"Yes, shoe-button eyes!" Raggedy Ann replied.

"I would tell you from the others by your dress, Raggedy Ann," said the French doll, "Your dress is fifty years old! I could tell you by that!"

"But my new sister rag dolls have dresses just like mine, for the Stranger Friend had cloth made especially for them exactly like mine."

"I know how we could tell you from the other rag dolls, even if you all look exactly alike!" said the Indian doll, who had been thinking for a long time.

"How?" asked Raggedy Ann with a laugh.

"By feeling your candy heart! If the doll has a candy heart then it is you, Raggedy Ann!"

Raggedy Ann laughed, "I am so glad you all love me as you do, but I am sure you would not be able to tell me from my new sisters, except that I am more worn, for each new rag doll has a candy heart, and on it is written, '*I love you*' just as is written on my own candy heart."

"And there are hundreds and hundreds of the new rag dolls?" asked the little penny dolls.

"Hundreds and hundreds of them, all named Raggedy Ann," replied Raggedy.

"Then," said the penny dolls, "we are indeed happy and proud for you! For wherever one of the new Raggedy Ann dolls goes there will go with it the love and happiness that *you* give to others."

RAGGEDY ANDY
STORIES

RAGGEDY ANDY
STORIES
Introducing the Little Rag
Brother of Raggedy Ann

Written & Illustrated by
JOHNNY GRUELLE

LITTLE SIMON
New York   London   Toronto   Sydney

TO
MARCELLA'S MAMA

Gainsville, Florida,
January 8, 1919.

Johnny Gruelle,
Care of P. F. Volland Company.
Chicago, Ill.

Dear Johnny:

WHEN I saw your Raggedy Ann books and dolls in a store near here, I went right in and bought one of each, and when I had read your introduction to "Raggedy Ann" I went right up to an old trunk in my own attic and brought down the doll I am sending you with this letter.

This doll belonged to my mother and she played with it when a little girl. She treasured it highly, I know, for she kept it until I came and then she gave it to me.

The fun that we two have had together I cannot begin to tell you, but often, like the little boy who went out into the garden to eat worms when all the world seemed blue and clouded, this doll and I went out under the arbor and had our little cry together. I can still feel it's soft rag arms (as I used to imagine) about me, and hear the words of comfort (also imaginary) that were whispered in my ear.

As you say in your Raggedy Ann book, "Fairyland must be filled with rag dolls, soft loppy rag dolls who go through all the beautiful adventures found there, nestling in the crook of a dimpled arm." I truly believe there is such a fairyland

and that rag dolls were first made there, or how else could they bring so much sunshine into a child's life?

All the little girls of my acquaintance have your Raggedy Ann book and doll, and for the happiness you have brought to them let me give to you the doll of all my dolls, the doll I loved most dearly.

May it prove to you a gift from Fairyland, bringing with it all the "wish come true" that you may wish and, if possible, add to the sunshine in your life.

My mother called the doll Raggedy Andy and it was by this name that I have always known him. Is it any wonder that I was surprised when I saw the title of your book?

Introduce Raggedy Andy to Raggedy Ann, dear Johnny. Let him share in the happiness of your household.

Sincerely yours,

Raggedy Andy's "Mama."

*   *   *   *   *

Wilton, Connecticut,
January 12, 1919.

Dear John:

Your letter brings many pleasant memories to my mind and takes me back to my childhood.

Living next door to us, when I was about four years old, was a little girl named Bessie; I cannot recall her last name.

When my mother made Raggedy Ann for me, Bessie's mother made a rag doll for her, for we two always played together; as I recall, there was no fence between our two houses.

Bessie's doll was made a day or so after Raggedy Ann, I think, though I am not quite certain which of the two dolls was made first. However, Bessie's doll was given the name of Raggedy Andy, and one of the two dolls was named after the other, so that their names would sound alike.

We children played with the two rag dolls most of the time until Bessie's family moved away—when I was eight or nine years old. They had faces just alike; the mother who made the first doll probably painted both doll faces. I do not remember just how Raggedy Andy was dressed, but I know he often wore dresses over his boy clothes when Bessie and I decided that he and Raggedy Ann should be sisters for the day.

You will remember I told you about Raggedy Andy long ago, John.

Isn't it strange that the two old rag dolls should come together after all these years? I wish Raggedy Andy's "Mama" had signed her name, for I should like to write to her. Perhaps there may be some way of finding her out.

Anyway, it seems to me you have the subject for another rag doll book, for Raggedy Andy must have had some wonderful adventures in his long life.

Yours lovingly,

Mom.

*   *   *   *   *

HOW RAGGEDY ANDY CAME

ONE day Daddy took Raggedy Ann down to his office and propped her up against some books upon his desk; he wanted to have her where he could see her cheery smile all day, for, as you must surely know, smiles and happiness are truly catching.

Daddy wished to catch a whole lot of Raggedy Ann's cheeriness and happiness and put all this down on paper, so that those who did not have Raggedy Ann dolls might see just how happy and smiling a rag doll can be.

So Raggedy Ann stayed at Daddy's studio for three or four days.

She was missed very, very much at home and Marcella really longed for her, but knew that Daddy was borrowing some of Raggedy Ann's sunshine, so she did not complain.

Raggedy Ann did not complain either, for in addition to the sunny, happy smile she always wore (it was painted on), Raggedy Ann had a candy heart, and of course no one (not even a rag doll) ever complains if they have such happiness about them.

One evening, just as Daddy was finishing his day's work, a messenger boy came with a package; a nice, soft lumpy package.

Daddy opened the nice, soft lumpy package and found a letter.

Gran'ma had told Daddy, long before this, that at the time Raggedy Ann was made, a neighbor lady had made a boy doll, Raggedy Andy, for her little girl, who always played with Gran'ma.

And when Gran'ma told Daddy this she wondered whatever had become of her little playmate and the boy doll, Raggedy Andy.

After reading the letter, Daddy opened the other package which had been inside the nice, soft, lumpy package and found—Raggedy Andy.

Raggedy Andy had been carefully folded up.

His soft, loppy arms were folded up in front of him and his soft, loppy legs were folded over his soft, loppy arms, and they were held this way by a rubber band.

Raggedy Andy must have wondered why he was being "done up" this way, but it could not have caused him any worry, for in between where his feet came over his face Daddy saw his cheery smile.

After slipping off the rubber band, Daddy smoothed out the wrinkles in Raggedy Andy's arms and legs.

Then Daddy propped Raggedy Ann and Raggedy Andy up against books on his desk, so that they sat facing each other; Raggedy Ann's shoe button eyes looking straight into the shoe button eyes of Raggedy Andy.

They could not speak—not right out before a real person—so they just sat there and smiled at each other.

Daddy could not help reaching out his hands and feeling their throats.

Yes! There was a lump in Raggedy Ann's throat, and there was a lump in Raggedy Andy's throat. A cotton lump, to be sure, but a lump nevertheless.

"So, Raggedy Ann and Raggedy Andy, that is why you cannot talk, is it?" said Daddy.

"I will go away and let you have your visit to yourselves, although it is good to sit and share your happiness by watching you."

Daddy then took the rubber band and placed it around Raggedy Ann's right hand, and around Raggedy Andy's right hand, so that when he had it fixed properly they sat and held each other's hands.

Daddy knew they would wish to tell each other all the wonderful things that had happened to them since they had parted more than fifty years before.

So, locking his studio door, Daddy left the two old rag dolls looking into each other's eyes.

The next morning, when Daddy unlocked his door and looked at his desk, he saw that Raggedy Andy had fallen over so that he lay with his head in the bend of Raggedy Ann's arm.

THE NURSERY DANCE

When Raggedy Andy was first brought to the nursery he was very quiet.

Raggedy Andy did not speak all day, but he smiled pleasantly to all the other dolls. There was Raggedy Ann, the French doll, Henny, the little Dutch doll, Uncle Clem, and a few others.

Some of the dolls were without arms and legs.

One had a cracked head. She was a nice doll, though, and the others all liked her very much.

All of them had cried the night Susan (that was her name) fell off the toy box and cracked her china head.

Raggedy Andy did not speak all day.

But there was really nothing strange about this fact, after all.

None of the other dolls spoke all day, either.

Marcella had played in the nursery all day and of course they did not speak in front of her.

Marcella thought they did, though, and often had them saying things which they really were not even thinking of.

For instance, when Marcella served water with sugar in it and little oyster crackers for "tea," Raggedy Andy was thinking of Raggedy Ann, and the French doll was thinking of one time when Fido was lost.

Marcella took the French doll's hand, and passed a cup of "tea" to Raggedy Andy, and said, "Mr. Raggedy Andy, will you have another cup of tea?" as if the French doll was talking.

And then Marcella answered for Raggedy Andy, "Oh, yes, thank you! It is so delicious!"

Neither the French doll nor Raggedy Andy knew what was going on, for they were thinking real hard to themselves.

Nor did they drink the tea when it was poured for them. Marcella drank it instead.

Perhaps this was just as well, for, most of the dolls were moist inside from the "tea" of the day before.

Marcella did not always drink all of the tea, often she poured a little down their mouths.

Sugar and water, if taken in small quantities, would not give the dolls colic, Marcella would tell them, but she did not know that it made their cotton, or sawdust insides, quite sticky.

Quite often, too, Marcella forgot to wash their faces after a "tea," and Fido would do it for them when he came into the nursery and found the dolls with sweets upon their faces.

Really, Fido was quite a help in this way, but he often missed the corners of their eyes and the backs of their necks where the "tea" would run and get sticky. But he did his best and saved his little Mistress a lot of work.

No, Raggedy Andy did not speak; he merely thought a great deal.

One can, you know, when one has been a rag doll as long as Raggedy Andy had. Years and years and years and years!

Even Raggedy Ann, with all her wisdom, did not really know how long Raggedy Andy and she had been rag dolls.

If Raggedy Ann had a pencil in her rag hand and Marcella guided it for her, Raggedy Ann could count up to ten— sometimes. But why should one worry one's rag head about one's age when all one's life has been one happy experience after another, with each day filled with love and sunshine?

Raggedy Andy did not know his age, but he remembered many things that had happened years and years and years ago, when he and Raggedy Ann were quite young.

It was of these pleasant times Raggedy Andy was thinking all day, and this was the reason he did not notice that Marcella was speaking for him.

Raggedy Andy could patiently wait until Marcella put all the dollies to bed and left them for the night, alone in the nursery.

The day might have passed very slowly had it not been for the happy memories which filled Raggedy Andy's cotton-stuffed head.

But he did not even fidget.

Of course, he fell out of his chair once, and his shoe button eyes went "Click!" against the floor, but it wasn't his fault. Raggedy Andy was so loppy he could hardly be placed in a chair so that he would stay, and Marcella jiggled the table.

Marcella cried for Raggedy Andy, "AWAA! AWAA!" and picked him up and snuggled him and scolded Uncle Clem for jiggling the table.

Through all this Raggedy Andy kept right on thinking his pleasant thoughts, and really did not know he had fallen from the chair.

You see how easy it is to pass over the little bumps of life if we are happy inside.

And so Raggedy Andy was quiet all day, and so the day finally passed.

Raggedy Andy was given one of Uncle Clem's clean white nighties and shared Uncle Clem's bed. Marcella kissed them all good night and left them to sleep until morning.

But as soon as she had left the room all the dolls raised up in their beds. When their little mistress' footsteps passed out of hearing, all the dollies jumped out of their beds and gathered around Raggedy Andy.

Raggedy Ann introduced them one by one and Raggedy Andy shook hands with each.

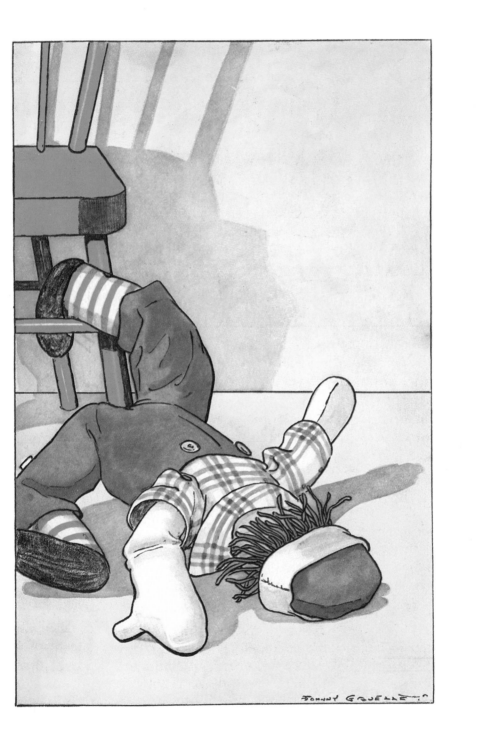

"I am very happy to know you all!" he said, in a voice as kindly as Raggedy Ann's, "and I hope we will all like each other as much as Raggedy Ann and I have always liked each other!"

"Oh, indeed we shall!" the dollies all answered. "We love Raggedy Ann because she is so kindly and happy, and we know we shall like you too, for you talk like Raggedy Ann and have the same cheery smile!"

"Now that we know each other so well, what do you say to a game, Uncle Clem?" Raggedy Andy cried, as he caught Uncle Clem and danced about the floor.

Henny, the Dutch doll, dragged the little square music box out into the center of the room and wound it up. Then all, catching hands, danced in a circle around it, laughing and shouting in their tiny doll voices.

"That was lots of fun!" Raggedy Andy said, when the music stopped and all the dolls had taken seats upon the floor facing him. "You know I have been shut up in a trunk up in an attic for years and years and years."

"Wasn't it very lonesome in the trunk all that time?"

Susan asked in her queer little cracked voice. You see, her head had been cracked.

"Oh, not at all," Raggedy Andy replied, "for there was always a nest of mice down in the corner of the trunk. Cute little Mama and Daddy mice, and lots of little teeny weeny baby mice. And when the mama and daddy mice were away, I used to cuddle the tiny little baby mice!"

"No wonder you were never lonesome!" said Uncle Clem, who was very kind and loved everybody and everything.

"No, I was never lonesome in the old trunk in the attic, but it is far more pleasant to be out again and living here with all you nice friends!" said Raggedy Andy.

And all the dolls thought so too, for already they loved Raggedy Andy's happy smile and knew he would prove to be as kindly and lovable as Raggedy Ann.

JOHNNY GRUELLE

THE SPINNING WHEEL

One night, after all the household had settled down to sleep, Raggedy Andy sat up in bed and tickled Uncle Clem.

Uncle Clem twisted and wiggled in his sleep until finally he could stand it no longer and awakened.

"I dreamed that some one told me the funniest story!" said Uncle Clem; "But I cannot remember what it was!"

"I was tickling you!" laughed Raggedy Andy.

When the other dolls in the nursery heard Raggedy Andy and Uncle Clem talking, they too sat up in their beds.

"We've been so quiet all day," said Raggedy Andy. "Let's have a good romp!"

This suggestion suited all the dolls, so they jumped out of their beds and ran over towards Raggedy Andy's and Uncle Clem's little bed.

Raggedy Andy, always in for fun, threw his pillow at Henny, the Dutch doll.

Henny did not see the pillow coming towards him so he was knocked head over heels.

Henny always said "Mama" when he was tilted backward or forward, and when the pillow rolled him over and over, he cried, "Mama, Mama, Mama!"

It was not because it hurt him, for you know Santa Claus always sees to it that each doll he makes in his great workshop is covered with a very magical Wish, and this Wish always keeps them from getting hurt.

Henny could talk just as well as any of the other dolls when he was standing up, sitting, or lying down, but if he was being tipped forward and backward, all he could say was, "Mama."

This amused Henny as much as it did the other dolls, so when he jumped to his feet he laughed and threw the pillow back at Raggedy Andy.

Raggedy Andy tried to jump to one side, but forgot that he was on the bed, and he and Uncle Clem went tumbling to the floor.

Then all the dolls ran to their beds and brought their pillows and had the jolliest pillow fight imaginable.

The excitement ran so high and the pillows flew so fast, the floor of the nursery was soon covered with feathers. It was only when all the dolls had stopped to rest and put the feathers back into the pillow cases that Raggedy Andy discovered he had lost one of his arms in the scuffle.

The dolls were worried over this and asked, "What will Marcella say when she sees that Raggedy Andy has lost an arm?"

"We can push it up his sleeve!" said Uncle Clem. "Then when Raggedy Andy is taken out of bed in the morning, Marcella will find his arm is loose!"

"It has been hanging by one or two threads for a day or more!" said Raggedy Andy. "I noticed the other day that sometimes my thumb was turned clear around to the back, and I knew then that the arm was hanging by one or two threads and the threads were twisted."

Uncle Clem pushed Raggedy Andy's arm up through his sleeve, but every time Raggedy Andy jumped about, he lost his arm again.

"This will never do!" said Raggedy Ann. "Raggedy Andy is lopsided with only one arm and he cannot join in our games as well as if he had two arms!"

"Oh, I don't mind that!" laughed Raggedy Andy. "Mar-

cella will sew it on in the morning and I will be all right, I'm sure!"

"Perhaps Raggedy Ann can sew it on now!" suggested Uncle Clem.

"Yes, Raggedy Ann can sew it on!" all the dolls cried. "She can play Peter, Peter, Pumpkin Eater on the toy piano and she can sew!"

"I will gladly try," said Raggedy Ann, "but there are no needles or thread in the nursery, and I have to have a thimble so the needle can be pressed through Raggedy Andy's cloth!"

"Marcella always gets a needle from Mama!" said the French Doll.

"I know," said Raggedy Ann, "but we cannot waken Mama to ask her!"

The dolls all laughed at this, for they knew very well that even had Mama been awake, they would not have asked her for needle and thread, because they did not wish her to know they could act and talk just like real people.

"Perhaps we can get the things out of the machine drawer!" Henny suggested.

"Yes," cried Susan, "let's all go get the things out of the machine drawer! Come on, everybody!"

And Susan, although she had only a cracked head, ran out the nursery door followed by all the rest of the dolls.

Even the tiny little penny dolls clicked their china heels upon the floor as they followed the rest, and Raggedy Andy, carrying his loose arm, thumped along in the rear.

Raggedy Andy had not lived in the house as long as the others; so he did not know the way to the room in which the machine stood.

After much climbing and pulling, the needle and thread and thimble were taken from the drawer, and all raced back again to the nursery.

Uncle Clem took off Raggedy Andy's waist, and the other dolls all sat around watching while Raggedy Ann sewed the arm on again.

Raggedy Ann had only taken two stitches when she began laughing so hard she had to quit. Of course when Raggedy Ann laughed, all the other dolls laughed too, for laughter, like yawning, is very catching.

"I was just thinking!" said Raggedy Ann. "Remember, 'way, 'way back, a long, long time ago, I sewed this arm on once before?" she asked Raggedy Andy.

"I do remember, now that you mention it," said Raggedy Andy, "but I can not remember how the arm came off!"

"Tell us about it!" all the dolls cried.

"Let's see!" Raggedy Ann began. "Your Mistress left you over at our house one night, and after everyone had gone to bed, we went up into the attic!"

"Oh, yes! I do remember now!" Raggedy Andy laughed. "We played with the large whirligig!"

"Yes," Raggedy Ann said. "The large spinning wheel. We held on to the wheel and went round and round! And when we were having the most fun, your feet got fastened between the wheel and the rod which held the wheel in position and there you hung, head down!"

"I remember, you were working the pedal and I was sailing around very fast," said Raggedy Andy, "and all of a sudden the wheel stopped!"

"We would have laughed at the time," Raggedy Ann explained to the other dolls, "but you see it was quite serious."

"My mistress had put us both to bed for the night, and if she had discovered us 'way up in the attic, she would have wondered how in the world we got there! So there was nothing to do but get Raggedy Andy out of the tangle!"

"But you pulled me out all right!" Raggedy Andy laughed.

"Yes, I pulled and I pulled until I pulled one of Raggedy Andy's arms off," Raggedy Ann said. "And then I pulled and pulled until finally his feet came out of the wheel and we both tumbled to the floor!"

"Then we ran downstairs as fast as we could and climbed into bed, didn't we!" Raggedy Andy laughed.

"Yes, we did!" Raggedy Ann replied. "And when we jumped into bed, we remembered that we had left Raggedy Andy's arm lying up on the attic floor, so we had to run back up there and get it! Remember, Raggedy Andy?"

"Yes! Wasn't it lots of fun?"

"Indeed it was!" Raggedy Ann agreed.

"Raggedy Andy wanted to let the arm remain off until the next morning, but I decided it would be better to have it sewed on, just as it had been when Mistress put us to bed. So, just like tonight, we went to the pincushion and found a needle and thread and I sewed it on for him!"

"There!" Raggedy Ann said, as she wound the thread around her hand and pulled, so that the thread broke near Raggedy Andy's shoulder. "It's sewed on again, good as new!"

"Thank you, Raggedy Ann!" said Raggedy Andy, as he threw the arm about Raggedy Ann's neck and gave her a hug.

"Now we can have another game!" Uncle Clem cried as he helped Raggedy Andy into his waist and buttoned it for him.

Just then the little Cuckoo Clock on the nursery wall went, "Whirrr!" the little door opened, and the little bird put out his head and cried, "Cuckoo! cuckoo! cuckoo! cuckoo!"

"No more games!" Raggedy Ann said. "We must be very quiet from now on. The folks will be getting up soon!"

"Last one in bed is a monkey!" cried Raggedy Andy.

There was a wild scramble as the dolls rushed for their beds, and Susan, having to be careful of her cracked head, was the monkey. So Raggedy Andy, seeing that Susan was slow about getting into her bed, jumped out and helped her.

Then, climbing into the little bed which Uncle Clem shared with him, he pulled the covers up to his eyes and, after pretending to snore a couple of times, he lay very quiet, thinking of the kindness of his doll friends about him, until Marcella came and took him down to breakfast.

And all the other dolls smiled at him as he left the room, for they were very happy to know that their little mistress loved him as much as they did.

THE TAFFY PULL

"I know how we can have a whole lot of fun!" Raggedy Andy said to the other dolls. "We'll have a taffy pull!"

"Do you mean crack the whip, Raggedy Andy?" asked the French doll.

"He means a tug of war, don't you, Raggedy Andy?" asked Henny.

"No," Raggedy Andy replied, "I mean a taffy pull!"

"If it's lots of fun, then show us how to play the game!" Uncle Clem said. "We like to have fun, don't we?" And Uncle Clem turned to all the other dolls as he asked the question.

"It really is not a game," Raggedy Andy explained. "You see, it is only a taffy pull.

"We take sugar and water and butter and a little vinegar and put it all on the stove to cook. When it has cooked until it strings 'way out when you dip some up in a spoon, or gets hard when you drop some of it in a cup of water, then it is candy.

"Then it must be placed upon buttered plates until it has cooled a little, and then each one takes some of the candy and pulls and pulls until it gets real white. Then it is called 'Taffy'."

"That will be loads of fun!" "Show us how to begin!"

"Let's have a taffy pull!" "Come on, everybody!" the dolls cried.

"Just one moment!" Raggedy Ann said. She had remained quiet before, for she had been thinking very hard, so hard, in fact, that two stitches had burst in the back of her rag head. The dolls, in their eagerness to have the taffy pull, were dancing about Raggedy Andy, but when Raggedy Ann spoke, in her soft cottony voice, they all quieted down and waited for her to speak again.

"I was just thinking," Raggedy Ann said, "that it would be very nice to have the taffy pull, but suppose some of the folks smell the candy while it is cooking."

"There is no one at home!" Raggedy Andy said. "I thought of that, Raggedy Ann. They have all gone over to Cousin Jenny's house and will not be back until day after tomorrow. I heard Mama tell Marcella."

"If that is the case, we can have the taffy pull and all the fun that goes with it!" Raggedy Ann cried, as she started for the nursery door.

After her ran all the dollies, their little feet pitter-patting across the floor and down the hall.

When they came to the stairway Raggedy Ann, Raggedy Andy, Uncle Clem and Henny threw themselves down the stairs, turning over and over as they fell.

The other dolls, having china heads, had to be much more careful; so they slid down the banisters, or jumped from one step to another.

Raggedy Ann, Raggedy Andy, Uncle Clem and Henny piled in a heap at the bottom of the steps, and by the time they had untangled themselves and helped each other up, the other dolls were down the stairs.

To the kitchen they all raced. There they found the fire in the stove still burning.

Raggedy Andy brought a small stew kettle, while the others brought the sugar and water and a large spoon. They could not find the vinegar and decided not to use it, anyway.

Raggedy Andy stood upon the stove and watched the candy, dipping into it every once in a while to see if it had cooked long enough, and stirring it with the large spoon.

At last the candy began to string out from the spoon when it was held above the stew kettle, and after trying a few drops in a cup of cold water, Raggedy Andy pronounced it "done."

Uncle Clem pulled out a large platter from the pantry, and Raggedy Ann dipped her rag hand into the butter jar and buttered the platter.

The candy, when it was poured into the platter, was a lovely golden color and smelled delicious to the dolls. Henny could not wait until it cooled; so he put one of his chamois skin hands into the hot candy.

Of course it did not burn Henny, but when he pulled his hand out again, it was covered with a great ball of candy, which strung out all over the kitchen floor and got upon his clothes.

Then too, the candy cooled quickly, and in a very short time Henny's hand was encased in a hard ball of candy. Henny couldn't wiggle any of his fingers on that hand and he was sorry he had been so hasty.

While waiting for the candy to cool, Raggedy Andy said, "We must rub butter upon our hands before we pull the candy, or else it will stick to our hands as it has done to Henny's hands and have to wear off!"

"Will this hard ball of candy have to wear off of my hand?" Henny asked. "It is so hard, I cannot wiggle any of my fingers!"

"It will either have to wear off, or you will have to soak your hand in water for a long time, until the candy on it melts!" said Raggedy Andy.

"Dear me!" said Henny.

Uncle Clem brought the poker then and, asking Henny to put his hand upon the stove leg, he gave the hard candy a few sharp taps with the poker and chipped the candy from Henny's hand.

"Thank you, Uncle Clem!" Henny said, as he wiggled his fingers. "That feels much better!"

Raggedy Andy told all the dolls to rub butter upon their hands.

"The candy is getting cool enough to pull!" he said.

Then, when all the dolls had their hands nice and buttery, Raggedy Andy cut them each a nice piece of candy and showed them how to pull it.

"Take it in one hand this way," he said, "and pull it with the other hand, like this!"

When all the dolls were supplied with candy they sat about and pulled it, watching it grow whiter and more silvery the longer they pulled.

Then, when the taffy was real white, it began to grow harder and harder, so the smaller dolls could scarcely pull it any more.

When this happened, Raggedy Andy, Raggedy Ann, Uncle Clem and Henny, who were larger, took the little dolls' candy and mixed it with what they had been pulling until all the taffy was snow white.

Then Raggedy Andy pulled it out into a long rope and held it while Uncle Clem hit the ends a sharp tap with the edge of the spoon.

This snipped the taffy into small pieces, just as easily as you might break icicles with a few sharp taps of a stick.

The small pieces of white taffy were placed upon the buttered platter again and the dolls all danced about it, singing and laughing, for this had been the most fun they had had for a long, long time.

"But what shall we do with it?" Raggedy Ann asked.

"Yes, what shall we do with it!" Uncle Clem said. "We can't let it remain in the platter here upon the kitchen floor! We must hide it, or do something with it!"

"While we are trying to think of a way to dispose of it, let us be washing the stew kettle and the spoon!" said practical Raggedy Ann.

"That is a very happy thought, Raggedy Ann!" said Raggedy Andy. "For it will clean the butter and candy from our hands while we are doing it!"

So the stew kettle was dragged to the sink and filled with water, the dolls all taking turns scraping the candy from the sides of the kettle, and scrubbing the inside with a cloth.

When the kettle was nice and clean and had been wiped dry, Raggedy Andy found a roll of waxed paper in the pantry upon one of the shelves.

"We'll wrap each piece of taffy in a nice little piece of paper," he said, "then we'll find a nice paper bag, and put all the pieces inside the bag, and throw it from the upstairs window when someone passes the house so that someone may have the candy!"

All the dolls gathered about the platter on the floor, and while Raggedy Andy cut the paper into neat squares, the dolls wrapped the taffy in the papers.

Then the taffy was put into a large bag, and with much pulling and tugging it was finally dragged up into the nursery, where a window faced out toward the street.

Then, just as a little boy and a little girl, who looked as though they did not ever have much candy, passed the house, the dolls all gave a push and sent the bag tumbling to the sidewalk.

The two children laughed and shouted, "Thank you," when they saw that the bag contained candy, and the dolls, peeping from behind the lace curtains, watched the two happy faced children eating the taffy as they skipped down the street.

When the children had passed out of sight, the dolls climbed down from the window.

"That was lots of fun!" said the French doll, as she smoothed her skirts and sat down beside Raggedy Andy.

"I believe Raggedy Andy must have a candy heart too, like Raggedy Ann!" said Uncle Clem.

"No!" Raggedy Andy answered, "I'm just stuffed with white cotton and I have no candy heart, but some day perhaps I shall have!"

"A candy heart is very nice!" Raggedy Ann said. (You know, she had one.) "But one can be just as nice and happy and full of sunshine without a candy heart."

"I almost forgot to tell you," said Raggedy Andy, "that when pieces of taffy are wrapped in little pieces of paper, just as we wrapped them, they are called 'Kisses'."

THE RABBIT CHASE

"Well, what shall we play tonight?" asked Henny, the Dutch doll, when the house was quiet and the dolls all knew that no one else was awake.

Raggedy Andy was just about to suggest a good game, when Fido, who sometimes slept in a basket in the nursery, growled.

All the dollies looked in his direction.

Fido was standing up with his ears sticking as straight in the air as loppy silken puppy dog ears can stick up.

"He must have been dreaming!" said Raggedy Andy.

"No, I wasn't dreaming!" Fido answered. "I heard something go, 'Scratch! Scratch!' as plain as I hear you!"

"Where did the sound come from, Fido?" Raggedy Andy asked when he saw that Fido really was wide awake.

"From outside somewhere!" Fido answered. "And if I could get out without disturbing all the folks, I'd run out and see what it might be! Perhaps I had better bark!"

"Please do not bark!" Raggedy Andy cried as he put his rag arm around Fido's nose. "You will awaken everybody in the house. We can open a door or a window for you and let you out, if you must go!"

"I wish you would. Listen! There it is again: 'Scratch! Scratch!' What can it be?"

"You may soon see!" said Raggedy Andy. "We'll let you out, but please don't sit at the door and bark and bark to get back in again, as you usually do, for we are going to play a good game and we may not hear you!"

"You can sleep out in the shed after you have found out what it is," said Raggedy Andy.

As soon as the dolls opened the door for Fido, he went running across the lawn, barking in a loud shrill voice. He ran down behind the shed and through the garden, and then back towards the house again.

Raggedy Andy and Uncle Clem stood looking out of the door, the rest of the dolls peeping over their shoulders, so when something came jumping through the door, it hit Uncle Clem and Raggedy Andy and sent them flying against the other dolls behind them.

All the dolls went down in a wiggling heap on the floor.

It was surprising that the noise and confusion did not waken Daddy and the rest of the folks, for just as the dolls were untangling themselves from each other and getting upon their feet, Fido came jumping through the door and sent the dolls tumbling again.

Fido quit barking when he came through the door.

"Which way did he go?" he asked, when he could get his breath.

"What was it?" Raggedy Andy asked in return.

"It was a rabbit!" Fido cried. "He ran right in here, for I could smell his tracks!"

"We could feel him!" Raggedy Andy laughed.

"I could not tell you which way he went!" Uncle Clem said, "Except I feel sure he came through the door and into the house!"

None of the dolls knew into which room the rabbit had run.

Finally, after much sniffing, Fido traced the rabbit to the nursery, where, when the dolls followed, they saw the rabbit crouching behind the rocking horse.

Fido whined and cried because he could not get to the rabbit and bite him.

"You should be ashamed of yourself, Fido!" cried Raggedy Ann. "Just see how the poor bunny is trembling!"

"He should not come scratching around our house if he doesn't care to be chased!" said Fido.

"Why don't you stay out in the woods and fields where you really belong?" Raggedy Andy asked the rabbit.

"I came to leave some Easter eggs!" the bunny answered in a queer little quavery voice.

"An Easter bunny!" all the dolls cried, jumping about and clapping their hands. "An Easter bunny!"

"Well!" was all Fido could say, as he sat down and began wagging his tail.

"You may come out from behind the rocking horse now, Easter bunny!" said Raggedy Andy. "Fido will not hurt you, now that he knows, will you, Fido?"

"Indeed I won't!" Fido replied. "I'm sorry that I chased you! And I remember now, I had to jump over a basket out by the shed! Was that yours?"

"Yes, it was full of Easter eggs and colored grasses for the little girl who lives here!" the bunny said.

When the Easter bunny found out that Fido and the dolls were his friends, he came out from behind the rocking horse and hopped across the floor to the door.

"I must go see if any of the eggs are broken, for if they are, I will have to run home and color some more! I was just about to make a nice nest and put the eggs in it when Fido came bouncing out at me!"

And with a squeeky little laugh the Easter bunny, followed by Fido and all the dolls, hopped across the lawn towards the shed. There they found the basket. Four of the lovely colored Easter eggs were broken.

"I will run home and color four more. It will only take a few minutes, so when I return and scratch again to make a nest, please do not bark at me!" said the Easter bunny.

"I won't! I promise!" Fido laughed.

"May we go with you and watch you color the Easter eggs?" Raggedy Andy begged.

"Indeed you may!" the Easter bunny answered. "Can you run fast?"

Then down through the garden and out through a crack in the fence the Easter bunny hopped, with a long string of dolls trailing behind.

When they came to the Easter bunny's home, they found Mama Easter bunny and a lot of little teeny weeny bunnies who would some day grow up to be big Easter bunnies like their Mama and Daddy bunny.

The Easter bunny told them of his adventure with Fido, and all joined in his laughter when they found it had turned out well at the end.

The Easter bunny put four eggs on to boil and while these were boiling he mixed up a lot of pretty colors.

When the eggs were boiled, he dipped the four eggs into the pretty colored dye and then painted lovely flowers on them.

When the Easter bunny had finished painting the eggs he put them in his basket and, with all the dolls running along beside him, they returned to the house.

"Why not make the nest right in the nursery?" Raggedy Andy asked.

"That would be just the thing! Then the little girl would wonder and wonder how I could ever get into the nursery without awakening the rest of the folks, for she will never suspect that you dolls and Fido let me in!"

So with Raggedy Andy leading the way, they ran up to the nursery and there, 'way back in a corner, they watched the Easter bunny make a lovely nest and put the Easter eggs in it.

And in the morning when Marcella came in to see the dolls you can imagine her surprise when she found the pretty gift of the Easter bunny.

"How in the world did the bunny get inside the house and into this room without awakening Fido?" she laughed.

And Fido, pretending to be asleep, slowly opened one eye and winked over the edge of his basket at Raggedy Andy.

And Raggedy Andy smiled back at Fido, but never said a word.

JOHNNY GRUELLE

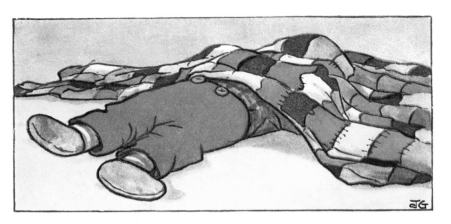

THE NEW TIN GUTTER

All day Saturday the men had worked out upon the eaves of the house and the dolls facing the window could see them.

The men made quite a lot of noise with their hammers, for they were putting new gutters around the eaves, and pounding upon tin makes a great deal of noise.

Marcella had not played with the dolls all that day, for she had gone visiting; so when the men hammered and made a lot of noise, the dolls could talk to each other without fear of anyone hearing or knowing they were really talking to each other.

"What are they doing now?" Raggedy Andy asked.

He was lying with his head beneath a little bed quilt, just as Marcella had dropped him when she left the nursery; so he could not see what was going on.

"We can only see the men's legs as they pass the window," answered Uncle Clem. "But they are putting new shingles or something on the roof!"

After the men had left their work and gone home to supper and the house was quiet, Raggedy Andy cautiously moved his head out from under the little bed quilt and, seeing that the coast was clear, sat up.

This was a signal for all the dolls to sit up and smooth out the wrinkles in their clothes.

The nursery window was open; so Raggedy Andy lifted the penny dolls to the sill and climbed up beside them.

Leaning out, he could look along the new shiny tin gutter the men had put in place.

"Here's a grand place to have a lovely slide!" he said as he gave one of the penny dolls a scoot down the shiny tin gutter.

"Whee! See her go!" Raggedy Andy cried.

All the other dolls climbed upon the window sill beside him.

"Scoot me too!" cried the other little penny doll in her squeeky little voice, and Raggedy Andy took her in his rag hand and gave her a great swing which sent her scooting down the shiny tin gutter, "Kerswish!"

Then Raggedy Andy climbed into the gutter himself and, taking a few steps, spread out his feet and went scooting down the shiny tin.

The other dolls followed his example and scooted along behind him.

When Raggedy Andy came to the place where he expected to find the penny dolls lying, they were nowhere about.

"Perhaps you scooted them farther than you thought!" Uncle Clem said.

"Perhaps I did!" Raggedy Andy said, "We will look around the bend in the eave!"

"Oh dear!" he exclaimed when he had peeped around the corner of the roof, "the gutter ends here and there is nothing but a hole!"

"They must have scooted right into the hole," Henny, the Dutch doll said.

Raggedy Andy lay flat upon the shiny tin and looked down into the hole.

"Are you down there, penny dolls?" he called.

There was no answer.

"I hope their heads were not broken!" Raggedy Ann said.

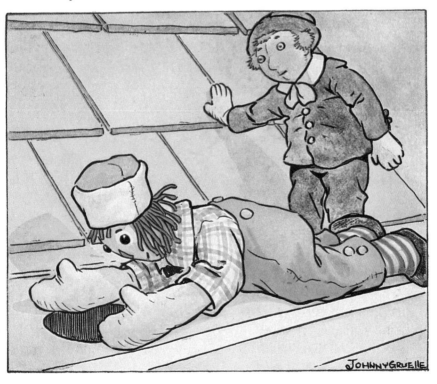

"I'm so sorry I scooted them!" Raggedy Andy cried, as he brushed his hand over his shoe button eyes.

"Maybe if you hold to my feet, I can reach down the hole and find them and pull them up again!" he added.

Uncle Clem and Henny each caught hold of a foot of Raggedy Andy and let him slide down into the hole.

It was a rather tight fit, but Raggedy Andy wiggled and twisted until all the dolls could see of him were his two feet.

"I can't find them!" he said in muffled tones. "Let me down farther and I think I'll be able to reach them!"

Now Henny and Uncle Clem thought that Raggedy Andy meant for them to let go of his feet and this they did.

Raggedy Andy kept wiggling and twisting until he came to a bend in the pipe and could go no farther.

"I can't find them!" he cried. "They have gone farther down the pipe! Now you can pull me up!"

"We can't reach you, Raggedy Andy!" Uncle Clem called down the pipe. "Try to wiggle back up a piece and we will catch your feet and pull you up!"

Raggedy Andy tried to wiggle backward up the pipe, but his clothes caught upon a little piece of tin which stuck out from the inside of the pipe and there he stayed. He could neither go down nor come back up.

"What shall we do?" Uncle Clem cried, "The folks will never find him down there, for we can not tell them where he is, and they will never guess it!"

The dolls were all very sad. They stayed out upon the shiny new tin gutter until it began raining and hoped and hoped that Raggedy Andy could get back up to them.

Then they went inside the nursery and sat looking out the window until it was time for the folks to get up and the house to be astir. Then they went back to the position each had been in, when Marcella had left them.

And although they were very quiet, each one was so sorry to lose Raggedy Andy, and each felt that he would never be found again.

JOHNNY GRUELLE.

"The rain must have soaked his cotton through and through!" sighed Raggedy Ann. "For all the water from the house runs down the shiny tin gutters and down the pipe into a rain barrel at the bottom!"

Then Raggedy Ann remembered that there was an opening at the bottom of the pipe.

"Tomorrow night if we have a chance, we dolls must take a stick and see if we can reach Raggedy Andy from the bottom of the pipe and pull him down to us!" she thought.

Marcella came up to the nursery and played all day, watching the rain patter upon the new tin gutter. She wondered where Raggedy Andy was, although she did not get worried about him until she had asked Mama where he might be.

"He must be just where you left him!" Mama said.

"I cannot remember where I left him!" Marcella said. "I thought he was with all the other dolls in the nursery, though!"

All day Sunday it rained and all of Sunday night, and Monday morning when Daddy started to work it was still raining.

As Daddy walked out of the front gate, he turned to wave good-bye to Mama and Marcella and then he saw something.

Daddy came right back into the house and called up the men who had put in the new shiny tin gutters.

"The drain pipe is plugged up. Some of you must have left shavings or something in the eaves, and it has washed down into the pipe, so that the water pours over the gutter in sheets!"

"We will send a man right up to fix it!" the men said.

So along about ten o'clock that morning one of the men came to fix the pipe.

But although he punched a long pole down the pipe, and punched and punched, he could not dislodge whatever it was which plugged the pipe and kept the water from running through it.

Then the man measured with his stick, so that he knew just where the place was, and with a pair of tin shears he cut a section from the pipe and found Raggedy Andy.

Raggedy Andy was punched quite out of shape and all jammed together, but when the man straightened out the funny little figure, Raggedy Andy looked up at him with his customary happy smile.

The man laughed and carried little water-soaked Raggedy Andy into the house.

"I guess your little girl must have dropped this rag doll down into the drain pipe!" the man said to Mama.

"I'm so glad you found him!" Mama said to the man.

"We have hunted all over the house for him! Marcella could not remember where she put him; so when I get him nice and dry, I'll hide him in a nice easy place for her to find, and she will not know he has been out in the rain all night!"

So Mama put Raggedy Andy behind the radiator and there he sat all afternoon, steaming and drying out.

And as he sat there he smiled and smiled, even though there was no one to see him.

He felt very happy within and he liked to smile, anyway, because his smile was painted on.

And another reason Raggedy Andy smiled was because he was not lonesome.

Inside his waist were the two little penny dolls.

The man had punched Raggedy Andy farther down into the pipe, and he had been able to reach the two little dolls and tuck them into a safe place.

"Won't they all be surprised to see us back again!" Raggedy Andy whispered as he patted the two little penny dolls with his soft rag hands.

And the two little penny dolls nestled against Raggedy Andy's soft cotton stuffed body, and thought how nice it was to have such a happy, sunny friend.

DOCTOR RAGGEDY ANDY

Raggedy Andy, Raggedy Ann, Uncle Clem and Henny were not given medicine.

Because, you see, they had no mouths.

That is, mouths through which medicine could be poured.

Their mouths were either painted on, or were sewed on with yarn.

Sometimes the medicine spoon would be touched to their faces but none of the liquid be given them. Except accidentally.

But the French doll had a lovely mouth for taking medicine; it was open and showed her teeth in a dimpling smile.

She also had soft brown eyes which opened and closed when she was tilted backward or forward.

The medicine which was given the dolls had great curing properties.

It would cure the most stubborn case of croup, measles, whooping cough or any other ailment the dolls had wished upon them by their little Mistress.

Some days all the dolls would be put to bed with "measles" but in the course of half an hour they would have every other ailment in the Doctor book.

The dolls enjoyed it very much, for, you see, Marcella always tried the medicine first to see if it was strong enough before she gave any to the dolls.

So the dolls really did not get as much of the medicine as their little mistress.

The wonderful remedy was made from a very old recipe handed down from ancient times.

This recipe is guaranteed to cure every ill a doll may have.

The medicine was made from brown sugar and water. Perhaps you may have used it for your dollies.

The medicine was also used as "tea" and "soda water," except when the dolls were supposed to be ill.

Having nothing but painted or yarn mouths, the ailments of Raggedy Andy, Raggedy Ann, Uncle Clem and Henny, the Dutch doll, mostly consisted of sprained wrists, arms and legs, or perhaps a headache and a toothache.

None of them knew they had the trouble until Marcella had wrapped up the "injured" rag arm, leg or head, and had explained in detail just what was the matter.

Raggedy Andy, Raggedy Ann, Uncle Clem, or Henny were just as happy with their heads tied up for the toothache as they were without their heads tied up.

Not having teeth, naturally they could not have the tooth-ache, and if they could furnish amusement for Marcella by having her pretend they had the toothache, then that made them very happy.

So this day, the French doll was quite ill. She started out with the "croup," and went through the "measles," "whooping cough," and "yellow fever" in an hour.

The attack came on quite suddenly.

The French doll was sitting quietly in one of the little red chairs, smiling the prettiest of dimpling smiles at Raggedy Andy, and thinking of the romp the dolls would have that night after the house grew quiet, when Marcella discovered that the French doll had the "croup" and put her to bed.

The French doll closed her eyes when put to bed, but the rest of her face did not change expression. She still wore her happy smile.

Marcella mixed the medicine very "strong" and poured it into the French doll's open mouth.

She was given a "dose" every minute or so.

It was during the "yellow fever" stage that Marcella was called to supper and left the dolls in the nursery alone.

Marcella did not play with them again that evening; so the dolls all remained in the same position until Marcella and the rest of the folks went to bed.

Then Raggedy Andy jumped from his chair and wound up the little music box. "Let's start with a lively dance!" he cried.

When the music started tinkling he caught the French doll's hand, and danced 'way across the nursery floor before he discovered that her soft brown eyes remained closed as they were when she lay upon the "sick" bed.

All the dolls gathered around Raggedy Andy and the French doll.

"I can't open my eyes!" she said.

Raggedy Andy tried to open the French doll's eyes with his soft rag hands, but it was no use.

They shook her. This sometimes has the desired effect when dolls do not open their eyes.

They shook her again and again. It was no use, her eyes remained closed.

"It must be the sticky, sugary 'medicine'!" said Uncle Clem.

"I really believe it must be!" the French doll replied. "The 'medicine' seemed to settle in the back of my head when I was lying down, and I can still feel it back there!"

"That must be it, and now it has hardened and keeps your pretty eyes from working!" said Raggedy Ann. "What shall we do?"

Raggedy Andy and Raggedy Ann walked over to a corner of the nursery and thought and thought. They pulled their foreheads down into wrinkles with their hands, so that they might think harder.

JOHNNY GRUELLE.

Finally Raggedy Ann cried, "I've thought of a plan!" and went skipping from the corner out to where the other dolls sat about the French doll.

"We must stand her upon her head, then the 'medicine' will run up into her hair, for there is a hole in the top of her head. I remember seeing it when her hair came off one time!"

"No sooner said than done!" cried Uncle Clem, as he took the French doll by the waist and stood her upon her head.

"That should be long enough!" Raggedy Ann said, when Uncle Clem had held the French doll in this position for five minutes.

But when the French doll was again placed upon her feet her eyes still remained tightly closed.

All this time, Raggedy Andy had remained in the corner, thinking as hard as his rag head would think.

He thought and thought, until the yarn hair upon his head stood up in the air and wiggled.

"If the 'medicine' did not run up into her hair when she stood upon her head," thought Raggedy Andy, "then it is because the 'medicine' could not run; so, if the medicine can not run, it is because it is too sticky and thick to run out the hole in the top of her head." He also thought a lot more.

At last he turned to the others and said out loud, "I can't seem to think of a single way to help her open her eyes unless we take off her hair and wash the medicine from inside her china head."

"Why didn't I think of that?" Raggedy Ann asked. "That is just the way we shall have to do!"

So Raggedy Ann caught hold of the French doll's feet, and Raggedy Andy caught hold of the French doll's lively curls, and they pulled and they pulled.

Then the other dolls caught hold of Raggedy Ann and Raggedy Andy and pulled and pulled, until finally, with a sharp "R-R-Rip!" the French doll's hair came off, and the dolls who were pulling went tumbling over backwards.

JOHNNY GRUELLE.

Laughingly they scrambled to their feet and sat the French doll up, so they might look into the hole in the top of her head.

Yes, the sticky "medicine" had grown hard and would not let the French doll's eyes open.

Raggedy Andy put his hand inside and pushed on the eyes so that they opened.

This was all right, only now the eyes would not close when the French doll lay down. She tried it.

So Raggedy Andy ran down into the kitchen and brought up a small tin cup full of warm water and a tiny rag.

With these he loosened the sticky "medicine" and washed the inside of the French doll's head nice and clean.

There were lots of cooky and cracker crumbs inside her head, too.

Raggedy Andy washed it all nice and clean, and then wet the glue which made the pretty curls stay on.

So when her hair was placed upon her head again, the French doll was as good as new.

"Thank you all very much!" she said, as she tilted backwards and forwards, and found that her eyes worked very easily.

Raggedy Andy again wound up the little music box and, catching the French doll about the waist, started a rollicking dance which lasted until the roosters in the neighborhood began their morning crowing.

Then, knowing the folks might soon be astir, the dolls left off their playing, and all took the same positions they had been in when Marcella left them the night before.

And so Marcella found them.

The French doll was in bed with her eyes closed, and her happy dimpling smile lighting up her pretty face.

And to this day, the dollies' little mistress does not know that Raggedy Andy was the doctor who cured the French doll of her only ill.

RAGGEDY ANDY'S SMILE

Raggedy Andy's smile was gone.

Not entirely, but enough so that it made his face seem onesided.

If one viewed Raggedy Andy from the left side, one could see his smile.

But if one looked at Raggedy Andy from the right side, one could not see his smile. So Raggedy Andy's smile was gone.

It really was not Raggedy Andy's fault.

He felt just as happy and sunny as ever.

And perhaps would not have known the difference had not the other dolls told him he had only one half of his cheery smile left.

Nor was it Marcella's fault. How was she to know that Dickie would feed Raggedy Andy orange juice and take off most of his smile?

And besides taking off one half of Raggedy Andy's smile, the orange juice left a great brown stain upon his face.

Marcella was very sorry when she saw what Dickie had done.

Dickie would have been sorry, too, if he had been more than two years old, but when one is only two years old, he has very few sorrows.

Dickie's only sorrow was that Raggedy Andy was taken from him, and he could not feed Raggedy Andy more orange juice.

Marcella kissed Raggedy Andy more than she did the rest of the dolls that night, when she put them to bed, and this made all the dolls very happy.

It always gave them great pleasure when any of their number was hugged and kissed, for there was not a selfish doll among them.

Marcella hung up a tiny stocking for each of the dollies, and placed a tiny little china dish for each of the penny dolls beside their little spool box bed.

For, as you probably have guessed, it was Christmas eve, and Marcella was in hopes Santa Claus would see the tiny stockings and place something in them for each dollie.

Then when the house was very quiet, the French doll told Raggedy Andy that most of his smile was gone.

"Indeed!" said Raggedy Andy. "I can still feel it! It must be there!"

"Oh, but it really is gone!" Uncle Clem said. "It was the orange juice!"

"Well, I still feel just as happy," said Raggedy Andy, "so let's have a jolly game of some sort! What shall it be?"

"Perhaps we had best try to wash your face!" said practical Raggedy Ann. She always acted as a mother to the other dolls when they were alone.

"It will not do a bit of good!" the French doll told Raggedy Ann, "for I remember I had orange juice spilled upon a nice white frock I had one time, and the stain would never come out!"

"That is too bad!" Henny, the Dutch doll, said. "We shall miss Raggedy Andy's cheery smile when he is looking straight at us!"

"You will have to stand on my right side, when you wish to see my smile!" said Raggedy Andy, with a cheery little chuckle 'way down in his soft cotton inside.

"But I wish everyone to understand," he went on, "that I am smiling just the same, whether you can see it or not!"

And with this, Raggedy Andy caught hold of Uncle Clem and Henny, and made a dash for the nursery door, followed by all the other dolls.

Raggedy Andy intended jumping down the stairs, head over heels, for he knew that neither he, Uncle Clem nor Henny would break anything by jumping down stairs.

But just as they got almost to the door, they dropped to the floor in a heap, for there, standing watching the whole performance, was a man.

All the dolls fell in different attitudes, for it would never do for them to let a real person see that they could act and talk just like real people.

Raggedy Andy, Uncle Clem and Henny stopped so suddenly they fell over each other and Raggedy Andy, being in the lead and pulling the other two, slid right through the door and stopped at the feet of the man.

A cheery laugh greeted this and a chubby hand reached down and picked up Raggedy Andy and turned him over.

Raggedy Andy looked up into a cheery little round face, with a little red nose and red cheeks, and all framed in white whiskers which looked just like snow.

Then the little round man walked into the nursery and picked up all the dolls and looked at them. He made no noise when he walked, and this was why he had taken the dolls by surprise at the head of the stairs.

The little man with the snow-white whiskers placed all the dolls in a row and from a little case in his pocket he took a tiny bottle and a little brush. He dipped the little brush in the tiny bottle and touched all the dolls' faces with it.

He had purposely saved Raggedy Andy's face until the last. Then, as all the dolls watched, the cheery little white-whiskered man touched Raggedy Andy's face with the magic liquid, and the orange juice stain disappeared, and in its place came Raggedy Andy's rosy cheeks and cheery smile.

And, turning Raggedy Andy so that he could face all the other dolls, the cheery little man showed him that all the other dolls had new rosy cheeks and newly-painted faces. They all looked just like new dollies. Even Susan's cracked head had been made whole.

Henny, the Dutch doll, was so surprised he fell over backward and said, "Squeek!"

When the cheery little man with the white whiskers heard this, he picked Henny up and touched him with the paint brush in the center of the back, just above the place where Henny had the little mechanism which made him say "Mama" when he was new. And when the little man touched Henny and tipped him forward and backward, Henny was just as good as new and said "Mama" very prettily.

Then the little man put something in each of the tiny doll stockings, and something in each of the little china plates for the two penny dolls.

Then, as quietly as he had entered, he left, merely turning at the door and shaking his finger at the dolls in a cheery, mischievous manner.

Raggedy Andy heard him chuckling to himself as he went down the stairs.

Raggedy Andy tiptoed to the door and over to the head of the stairs.

Then he motioned for the other dolls to come.

There, from the head of the stairs, they watched the cheery little white-whiskered man take pretty things from a large sack and place them about the chimneyplace.

"He does not know that we are watching him," the dolls all thought, but when the little man had finished his task, he turned quickly and laughed right up at the dolls, for he had known that they were watching him all the time.

Then, again shaking his finger at them in his cheery manner, the little white-whiskered man swung the sack to his shoulder, and with a whistle such as the wind makes when it plays through the chinks of a window, he was gone—up the chimney.

The dolls were very quiet as they walked back into the nursery and sat down to think it all over, and as they sat there thinking, they heard out in the night the "tinkle, tinkle, tinkle" of tiny sleigh bells, growing fainter and fainter as they disappeared in the distance.

Without a word, but filled with a happy wonder, the dolls climbed into their beds, just as Marcella had left them, and pulled the covers up to their chins.

And Raggedy Andy lay there, his little shoe button eyes looking straight towards the ceiling and smiling a joyful smile—not a "half smile" this time, but a "full size smile."

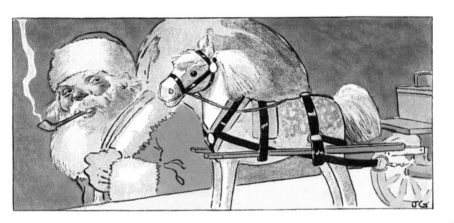

THE WOODEN HORSE

Santa Claus left a whole lot of toys.

A wooden horse, covered with canton flannel and touched lightly with a paint brush dipped in black paint to give him a dappled gray appearance, was one of the presents.

With the wooden horse came a beautiful red wagon with four yellow wheels. My! The paint was pretty and shiny.

The wooden horse was hitched to the wagon with a patent leather harness; and he, himself, stood proudly upon a red platform running on four little nickel wheels.

It was true that the wooden horse's eyes were as far apart as a camel's and made him look quite like one when viewed from in front, but he had soft leather ears and a silken mane and tail.

He was nice to look upon, was the wooden horse. All the dolls patted him and smoothed his silken mane and felt his shiny patent leather harness the first night they were alone with him in the nursery.

The wooden horse had a queer voice; the dolls could hardly understand him at first, but when his bashfulness wore off, he talked quite plainly.

"It is the first time I have ever tried to talk," he explained when he became acquainted, "and I guess I was talking down in my stomach instead of my head!"

"You will like it here in the nursery very much!" said Raggedy Andy. "We have such jolly times and love each other so much I know you will enjoy your new home!"

"I am sure I shall!" the wooden horse answered. "Where I came from, we—the other horses and myself—just stood silently upon the shelves and looked and looked straight ahead, and never so much as moved our tails."

"See if you can move your tail now!" Henny, the Dutch doll, suggested.

The wooden horse started to roll across the nursery floor and if Raggedy Ann had not been in the way, he might have bumped into the wall. As it was, the wooden horse rolled against Raggedy Ann and upset her but could go no further when his wheels ran against her rag foot.

When the wooden horse upset Raggedy Ann, he stood still until Uncle Clem and Henny and Raggedy Andy lifted him off Raggedy Ann's feet. "Did I frisk my tail?" he asked when Raggedy Ann stood up and smoothed her apron.

"Try it again!" said Raggedy Ann. "I couldn't see!" She laughed her cheery rag doll laugh, for Raggedy Ann, no matter what happened, never lost her temper.

The wooden horse started rolling backward at this and knocked Henny over upon his back, causing him to cry "Mama!" in his squeeky voice.

Uncle Clem, Raggedy Ann, and the tin soldier all held to the wooden horse and managed to stop him just as he was backing out of the nursery door towards the head of the stairs.

Then the dolls pulled the wooden horse back to the center of the room. "It's funny" he said, "that I start moving backward or forward when I try to frisk my tail!"

"I believe it is because you have stood so long upon the shelf without moving," Raggedy Andy suggested. "Suppose you try moving forward!"

Uncle Clem, who was standing in front of the wooden horse, jumped to one side so hastily his feet slipped out from under him, just as if he had been sliding upon slippery ice.

JOHNNY GRUELLE.

The wooden horse did not start moving forward as Uncle Clem had expected; instead, his silken tail frisked gaily up over his back.

"Whee! There, you frisked your tail!" cried all the dolls as joyfully as if the wooden horse had done something truly wonderful.

"It's easy now!" said the wooden horse. "When I wish to go forward or backward I'll try to frisk my tail and then I'll roll along on my shiny wheels; then when I wish to frisk my tail I'll try to roll forward or backward, like this!" But instead of rolling forward, the wooden horse frisked his tail. "I wanted to frisk my tail then!" he said in surprise. "Now I'll roll forward!" And sure enough, the wooden horse rolled across the nursery floor.

When he started rolling upon his shiny wheels, Raggedy Andy cried, "All aboard!" and, taking a short run, he leaped upon the wooden horse's back. Uncle Clem, Raggedy Ann, Henny, the Dutch doll and Susan, the doll without a head, all scrambled up into the pretty red wagon.

The wooden horse thought this was great fun and round

and round the nursery he circled. His shiny wheels and the pretty yellow wheels of the red wagon creaked so loudly none of the dolls heard the cries of the tiny penny dolls who were too small to climb aboard. Finally, as the wagon load of dolls passed the penny dolls, Raggedy Andy noticed the two little midgets standing together and missing the fun; so, leaning 'way over to one side as the horse swept by them, Raggedy Andy caught both the penny dolls in his strong rag arms and lifted them to a seat upon the broad back of the wooden horse.

"Hooray!" cried all the dolls when they saw Raggedy Andy's feat. "It was just like a Wild West Show!"

"We must all have all the fun we can together!" said Raggedy Andy.

"Good for you!" cried Uncle Clem. "The more fun we can give each other, the more fun each one of us will have!"

The wooden horse made the circle of the nursery a great
many times, for it pleased him very much to hear the gay
laughter of the dolls and he thought to himself, "How happy
I will be, living with such a jolly crowd."

But just as he was about to pass the door, there was a noise
upon the stairs and the wooden horse, hearing it, stopped so
suddenly Raggedy Andy and the penny dolls went clear over
his head and the dolls in the front of the wagon took Raggedy
Andy's seat upon the horse's back.

They lay just as they fell, for they did not wish anyone to
suspect that they could move or talk.

"Ha! Ha! Ha! I knew you were having a lot of fun!"
cried a cheery voice.

At this, all the dolls immediately scrambled back into
their former places, for they recognized the voice of the
French dollie.

But what was their surprise to see her dressed in a lovely
fairy costume, her lovely curls flying out behind, as she ran
towards them.

Raggedy Andy was just about to climb upon the horse's

back again when the French doll leaped there herself and, balancing lightly upon one foot, stood in this position while the wooden horse rolled around the nursery as fast as he could go.

Raggedy Andy and the two penny dolls ran after the wagon and, with the assistance of Uncle Clem and Raggedy Ann, climbed up in back.

When the wooden horse finally stopped the dolls all said, "This is the most fun we have had for a *long* time!"

The wooden horse, a thrill of happiness running through his wooden body, cried, "It is the most fun I have *ever* had!"

And the dolls, while they did not tell him so, knew that he had had the most fun because he had given *them* the most pleasure.

For, as you must surely know, they who are the most unselfish are the ones who gain the greatest joy; because they give happiness to others.

MAKING "ANGELS" IN THE SNOW

"Whee! It's good to be back home again!" said Raggedy Andy to the other dolls, as he stretched his feet out in front of the little toy stove and rubbed his rag hands briskly together, as if to warm them.

All the dolls laughed at Raggedy Andy for doing this, for they knew there had never been a fire in the little toy stove in all the time it had been in the nursery. And that was a long time.

"We are so glad and happy to have you back home again with us!" the dolls told Raggedy Andy. "For we have missed you very, very much!"

"Well," Raggedy Andy replied, as he held his rag hands over the tiny lid of the stove and rubbed them again, "I have missed all of you, too, and wished many times that you had been with me to join in and share in the pleasures and frolics I've had."

And as Raggedy Andy continued to hold his hands over the little stove, Uncle Clem asked him why he did it.

Raggedy Andy smiled and leaned back in his chair. "Really," he said, "I wasn't paying any attention to what I was doing! I've spent so much of my time while I was away drying out my soft cotton stuffing it seems as though it has almost become a habit."

"Were you wet most of the time, Raggedy Andy?" the French doll asked.

"Nearly all the time!" Raggedy Andy replied. "First I would get sopping wet and then I'd freeze!"

"Freeze!" exclaimed all the dolls in one breath.

"Dear me, yes!" Raggedy Andy laughed. "Just see here!" And Raggedy Andy pulled his sleeve up and showed where his rag arm had been mended. "That was quite a rip!" he smiled.

"Dear! Dear! How in the world did it happen? On a nail?" Henny, the Dutch doll, asked as he put his arm about Raggedy Andy.

"Froze!" said Raggedy Andy.

The dolls gathered around Raggedy Andy and examined the rip in his rag arm.

"It's all right now!" he laughed. "But you should have seen me when it happened! I was frozen into one solid cake of ice all the way through, and when Marcella tried to limber up my arm before it had thawed out, it went, 'Pop!' and just bursted.

"Then I was placed in a pan of nice warm water until the icy cotton inside me had melted, and then I was hung up on a line above the kitchen stove, out at Gran'ma's."

"But how did you happen to get so wet and then freeze?" asked Raggedy Ann.

"Out across the road from Gran'ma's home, 'way out in the country, there is a lovely pond," Raggedy Andy explained. "In the summer time pretty flowers grow about the edge, the little green frogs sit upon the pond lilies and beat upon their tiny drums all through the night, and the twinkling stars wink at their reflections in the smooth water. But when Marcella and I went out to Gran'ma's, last week, Gran'ma met us with a sleigh, for the ground was covered with starry snow. The pretty pond was covered with ice, too, and upon the ice was a soft blanket of the white, white snow. It was beautiful!" said Raggedy Andy.

"Gran'ma had a lovely new sled for Marcella, a red one with shiny runners.

"And after we had visited Gran'ma a while, we went to the pond for a slide.

"It was heaps of fun, for there was a little hill at one end of the pond so that when we coasted down, we went scooting across the pond like an arrow.

"Marcella would turn the sled sideways, just for fun, and she and I would fall off and go sliding across the ice upon our backs, leaving a clean path of ice, where we pushed aside the snow as we slid. Then Marcella showed me how to make 'angels' in the soft snow!"

"Oh, tell us how, Raggedy Andy!" shouted all the dollies.

"It's very easy!" said Raggedy Andy. "Marcella would lie down upon her back in the snow and put her hands back up over her head, then she would bring her hands in a circle down to her sides, like this." And Raggedy Andy lay upon the floor of the nursery and showed the dollies just how it was done. "Then," he added, "when she stood up it would leave the print of her body and legs in the white, white snow, and where she had swooped her arms there were the 'angel's wings!' "

"It must have looked just like an angel!" said Uncle Clem.

"Indeed it was very pretty!" Raggedy Andy answered. "Then Marcella made a lot of 'angels' by placing me in the snow and working my arms; so you see, what with falling off the sled so much and making so many 'angels,' we both were wet, but I was completely soaked through. My cotton just became soppy and I was ever so much heavier! Then Gran'ma, just as we were having a most delightful time, came to the door and 'Ooh-hooed' to Marcella to come and get a nice new doughnut. So Marcella, thinking to return in a minute, left me lying upon the sled and ran through the snow to Gran'ma's. And there I stayed and stayed until I began to feel stiff and could hear the cotton inside me go, 'Tic! Tic!' as it began to freeze.

"I lay upon the sled until after the sun went down. Two little Chicadees came and sat upon the sled and talked to me in their cute little bird language, and I watched the sky in the west get golden red, then turn into a deep crimson purple and finally a deep blue, as the sun went farther down around the bend of the earth. After it had been dark for some time, I heard someone coming through the snow and could see the yellow light of a lantern. It was Gran'ma.

"She pulled the sled over in back of her house and did not see that I was upon it until she turned to go in the kitchen; then she picked me up and took me inside. 'He's frozen as stiff as a board!' she told Marcella as she handed me to her. Marcella did not say why she had forgotten to come for me, but I found out afterward that it was because she was so wet. Gran'ma made her change her clothes and shoes and stockings and would not permit her to go out and play again.

"Well, anyway," concluded Raggedy Andy, "Marcella tried to limber my arm and, being almost solid ice, it just burst. And that is the way it went all the time we were out at Gran'ma's; I was wet nearly all the time. But I wish you could all have been with me to share in the fun."

And Raggedy Andy again leaned over the little toy stove and rubbed his rag hands briskly together.

Uncle Clem went to the waste paper basket and came back with some scraps of yellow and red paper. Then, taking off one of the tiny lids, he stuffed the paper in part of the way as if the flames were "shooting up!"

Then, as all the dolls' merry laughter rang out, Raggedy Andy stopped rubbing his hands, and catching Raggedy Ann about the waist, he went skipping across the nursery floor with her, whirling so fast neither saw they had gone out through the door until it was too late. For coming to the head of the stairs, they both went head over heels, "blumpity, blump!" over and over, until they wound up, laughing, at the bottom.

"Last one up is a Cocoa baby!" cried Raggedy Ann, as she scrambled to her feet. And with her skirts in her rag hands she went racing up the stairs to where the rest of the dollies stood laughing.

"Hurrah, for Raggedy Ann!" cried Raggedy Andy generously. "She won!"

THE SINGING SHELL

For years and years the beautiful shell had been upon the floor in Gran'ma's front room. It was a large shell with many points upon it. These were coarse and rough, but the shell was most beautiful inside.

Marcella had seen the shell time and time again and often admired its lovely coloring, which could be seen when one looked inside the shell.

So one day, Gran'ma gave the beautiful shell to Marcella to have for her very own, up in the nursery.

"It will be nice to place before the nursery door so the wind will not blow the door to and pinch anyone's fingers!" Gran'ma laughed.

So Marcella brought the shell home and placed it in front of the nursery door. Here the dolls saw it that night, when all the house was still, and stood about it wondering what kind of toy it might be.

"It seems to be nearly all mouth!" said Henny, the Dutch doll. "Perhaps it can talk."

"It has teeth!" the French doll pointed out. "It may bite!"

"I do not believe it will bite," Raggedy Andy mused, as he got down upon his hands and knees and looked up into the shell. "Marcella would not have it up here if it would bite!"

And, saying this, Raggedy Andy put his rag arm into the lovely shell's mouth.

"It doesn't bite! I knew it wouldn't!" he cried. "Just feel how smooth it is inside!"

All the dolls felt and were surprised to find it polished so highly inside, while the outside was so coarse and rough. With the help of Uncle Clem and Henny, Raggedy Andy turned the shell upon its back, so that all the dolls might look in.

The coloring consisted of dainty pinks, creamy whites and pale blues, all running together just as the coloring in an opal runs from one shade into another. Raggedy Andy, stooping over to look further up inside the pretty shell, heard something.

"It's whispering!" he said, as he raised up in surprise.

All the dolls took turns putting their ears to the mouth of the beautiful shell. Yes, truly it whispered, but they could not catch just what it said.

Finally Raggedy Andy suggested that all the dolls lie down upon the floor directly before the shell and keep very quiet.

"If we don't make a sound we may be able to hear what it says!" he explained.

So the dolls lay down, placing themselves flat upon the floor directly in front of the shell and where they could see and admire its beautiful coloring.

Now the dolls could be very, very quiet when they really wished to be, and it was easy for them to hear the faint whispering of the shell.

This is the story the shell told the dolls in the nursery that night:

"A long, long time ago, I lived upon the yellow sand, deep down beneath the blue, blue waters of the ocean. Pretty silken sea weeds grew around my home and reached their waving branches up, up towards the top of the water.

"Through the pretty sea weeds, fishes of pretty colors and shapes darted here and there, playing at their games.

It was still and quiet 'way down where I lived, for even if the ocean roared and pounded itself into an angry mass of tumbling waves up above, this never disturbed the calm waters down where I lived.

"Many times, little fishes or other tiny sea people came and hid within my pretty house when they were being pursued by larger sea creatures. And it always made me very happy to give them this protection.

"They would stay inside until I whispered that the larger creature had gone, then they would leave me and return to their play.

"Pretty little sea horses with slender, curving bodies often went sailing above me, or would come to rest upon my back. It was nice to lie and watch the tiny things curl their little tails about the sea weed and talk together, for the sea horses like one another and are gentle and kind to each other, sharing their food happily and smoothing their little ones with their cunning noses.

"But one day a diver leaped over the side of a boat and came swimming head-first down, down to where I lay. My! How the tiny sea creatures scurried to hide from him. He took me within his hand and, giving his feet a thump upon the yellow sand, rose with me to the surface.

"He poured the water from me, and out came all the little creatures who had been hiding there!"

Raggedy Andy wiggled upon the floor, he was so interested.

"Did the tiny creatures get back into the water safely?" he asked the beautiful shell.

"Oh, yes!" the shell whispered in reply. "The man held me over the side of the boat, so the tiny creatures went safely back into the water!"

"I am so glad!" Raggedy Andy said, with a sigh of relief. "He must have been a kindly man!"

"Yes, indeed!" the beautiful shell replied. "So I was placed along with a lot of other shells in the bottom of the boat and every once in a while another shell was placed amongst us. We whispered together and wondered where we were going. We were finally sold to different people and I have been at Gran'ma's house for a long, long time."

"You lived there when Gran'ma was a little girl, didn't you?" Raggedy Ann asked.

"Yes," replied the shell, "I have lived there ever since Gran'ma was a little girl. She often used to play with me and listen to me sing."

"Raggedy Ann can play 'Peter, Peter, Pumpkin Eater' on the piano, with one hand," said Uncle Clem, "but none of us can sing. Will you sing for us?" he asked the shell.

"I sing all the time," the shell replied, "for I cannot help singing, but my singing is a secret and so is very soft and low. Put your head close to the opening in my shell and listen!"

The dolls took turns doing this, and heard the shell sing softly and very sweetly.

"How strange and far away it sounds!" exclaimed the French doll. "Like fairies singing in the distance! The shell must be singing the songs of the mermaids and the water-fairies!"

"It is queer that anything so rough on the outside could be so pretty within!" said Raggedy Andy. "It must be a great pleasure to be able to sing so sweetly!"

"Indeed it is," replied the beautiful shell, "and I get a great happiness from singing all the time."

"And you will bring lots of pleasure to us, by being so happy!" said Raggedy Andy. "For although you may not enter into our games, we will always know that you are happily singing, and that will make us all happy!"

"I will tell you the secret of my singing," said the shell. "When anyone puts his ear to me and listens, he hears the reflection of his own heart's music, singing; so, you see, while I say that I am singing all the time, in reality I sing only when someone full of happiness hears his own singing as if it were mine."

"How unselfish you are to say this!" said Raggedy Andy. "Now we are ever so much more glad to have you with us. Aren't we?" he asked, turning to the rest of the dolls.

"Yes, indeed!" came the answer from all the dolls, even the tiny penny dolls.

"That is why the shell is so beautiful inside!" said Raggedy Ann. "Those who are unselfish may wear rough clothes, but inside they are always beautiful, just like the shell, and reflect to others the happiness and sunny music within their hearts!"

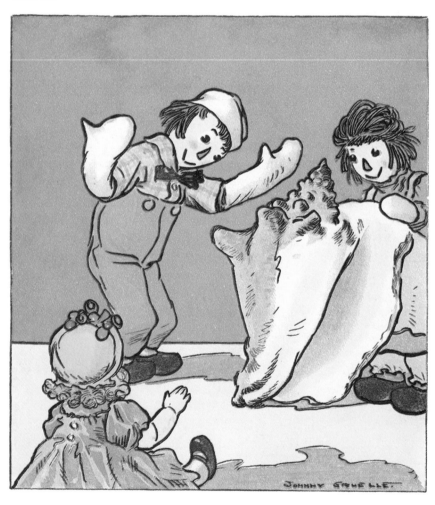

AFTERWORD
Johnny Gruelle and His Beloved Raggedys

"A rich man is one who spends his life in kindness making friends."
—*Johnny Gruelle*

My grandfather, Johnny Gruelle, lived as he wrote and believed. He was always a child at heart. His books contained nothing to cause fright, glorify mischief, excuse malice, or condone cruelty.

John Barton Gruelle was born Christmas morning, 1880, in Arcola, Illinois, the oldest son of Richard Buckner and Alice Gruelle. Richard, or R.B. as friends called him, was a self-taught landscape painter. When Johnny was two, the family moved to Indianapolis, which was becoming a cultural mecca for artists, writers, and musicians. There the Gruelle family soon became friends with other inspired midwestern artists, and R.B. became a member of the Hoosier Five artist group at this time.

R.B. and Alice saw to it that Johnny and their other children, Prudence and Justin, were exposed to art, literature, and music, and gave them ample opportunities for artistic expression. R. B. allowed the children to experiment freely with the paints and brushes in his home studio, and young Johnny often accompanied his father on landscape painting field trips. No doubt these outings to commune with nature, mixed with lively storytelling and music, instilled in Johnny the power of the written word and a strong appreciation of art for the heart's sake.

In 1903 Johnny was hired as an illustrator for the *Indianapolis Star*. Before long the managing editor recognized Johnny's talent for capturing, in pen and ink, the subtleties and whimsy of everyday life and put Johnny's political cartoons on the *Star*'s front page.

Talent as a cartoonist eventually led Johnny to the *Cleveland Press*. In 1910 at the advice of family and friends, Johnny entered a national competition sponsored by the *New York Herald*, which was seeking a new cartoonist for their Sunday color installment. Johnny's two submissions won first and second place in a blind competition of 1,500 entries. Johnny's first-place entry, "Mr. Twee Deedle" ran for ten years in the *New York Herald*.

Johnny and his wife Myrtle and young daughter, Marcella, relocated to the Norwalk, Connecticut, area. There they built a home for themselves in the Silvermine Artists Colony, not far from Johnny's mother and father, who had moved there earlier.

Using the tried and true techniques of the traditional storyteller, Johnny not only created new, whimsical tales for children, but also created many of the still-prevailing tales about his own life. He also initiated many legends about the genesis of Raggedy Ann and Andy, weaving fanciful details into factual accounts. With the wink of his eye or a flick of his pen, Johnny delighted in transporting all ages to the land of magic and make-believe. This affinity, coupled with his deeply spiritual connection to nature, magic, and all living things, enabled Johnny to create stories and illustrations that are just as loved today as they were when first created.

During 1914–1917 Johnny illustrated a comprehensive edition of Grimms' fairy tales for Cupples and Leon Publishers, and in 1917 wrote and illustrated his own book of original fairy tales, *My Very Own Fairy Stories*, published by P.F. Volland Co. He set many of these tales in a nursery full of dolls, giving each a whimsical name and a personality all its own. One of the dolls—one that would eventually star in her own books of tales—was Raggedy Ann. A doll that he created and patented in 1915, she was Marcella Gruelle's favorite. Around this time Marcella had fallen gravely ill from a contaminated vaccination. Her health slowly deteriorated until her death two years later. Johnny and Myrtle's second-born, Worth (my father), was just four years old at this time. He remembers his big sister with great love, and recollects his mother reading the stories that later became part of the "Raggedy" series of books. Worth's brother Richard was born in 1917 and the first edition of Johnny Gruelle's *Raggedy Ann Stories* was published in 1918. The book was such a hit that Johnny continued to write, illustrate, and have published at least one book a year in the Raggedy Ann and Andy series until his untimely death in 1938.

It is with great pleasure, tradition, and love that I see my grandfather's books back in print again in their original format, to be shared with generations of "Raggedy" lovers past, present, and future.

—Kim Gruelle